GLACIER BIGFOOT
CAMPFIRE STORIES

GLACIER BIGFOOT CAMPFIRE STORIES

RUSTY WILSON

ISBN: 978-1-948859-15-8

For Joe L.
And for all who love adventure, mystery, and the beautiful
wilderness of Glacier National Park

CONTENTS

FOREWORD

Ever thought about visiting beautiful Glacier National Park? The park is famous for its dramatic hiking and backpacking, but you might want to be sure you learn about the flora and fauna before you go, especially the fauna, which can also be quite dramatic.

It's best to go prepared, and these all new stories will help you be aware of what you might encounter out there, far from civilization and other people and, well, maybe even from possible rescue. This book also includes two excerpts from Rusty's *Montana Bigfoot Campfire Stories*.

Fly-fishing guide Rusty Wilson, known as the World's Greatest Bigfoot Story Teller, has spent years collecting these tales from his clients around the campfire, stories guaranteed to make sure you won't want to go out after dark.

Come join a disgruntled high-school kid and his flatlander uncle in their first-ever backpacking trip, one they're sure to never forget, then come along with a young girl who nearly loses her life in one of the park's icy streams, then faces ridicule because of how she was rescued. Join an artist as he experiences a strange mind-control game high on a dreamy pass, and if you live to tell about all that, come visit a fire lookout tower, where the lookout finds that he prefers spotting fires over spotting strange creatures.

Still have your wits about you? Read about an "imaginary" young Sasquatch "cub" found injured in the woods, and if that's not enough to make you shake your head, join a park ranger as he's nearly trapped in a tunnel through one of Glacier's high arêtes. Or how about getting caught in a Sasquatch rock fight along the trail to one of the park's hike-in chalets? And wait—a Bigfoot doctor?

You'll want to be sure you're not alone in the woods while reading these stories, and the audio book will keep you entertained as you drive those lonely backroads at night—just don't panic and run off the road!

Another great book from Rusty Wilson, Bigfoot expert and story-teller—tales for both the Bigfoot believer and for those who just enjoy a good story.

INTRODUCTION

Greetings, fellow adventurers, to another collection of Bigfoot camp-fire stories featuring one of our country's most beautiful places—Glacier National Park, known as the Crown of the Continent for its beauty.

Glacier preserves 1.2 million acres, most of which are accessible only by foot, and much of the area looks like it did when the Black-feet roamed the region many years ago. It's a wild ecosystem in an untouched landscape with 762 lakes (only 131 which are named), 175 mountains, and 563 streams.

And it's also a landscape with lots of Bigfoot, from what I can tell, for it borders even more wilderness in Canada. The western part of Glacier, the Northern Flathead Valley, has been called the single most important basin for carnivores in the Rocky Mountains. Whether Bigfoot should be classified as a carnivore or not remains to be seen, but the region makes great habitat for these large primates, sighted throughout the area since the days the Blackfeet and other natives hunted and roamed the area.

My home base is Colorado, though I often go to Montana for part of the summer as a fishing guide. Ironically, though the stories happened in Glacier, I collected the majority of them in Colorado, most from around campfires with my fly-fishing clients, though some were told to me in private. I'm always very careful to select stories that I believe to be authentic, though how would I ever know without actually being there?

So, sit back with a cup of hot chocolate in a big comfy chair or by a campfire and enjoy. Get out a map and follow along, and if you ever get the chance to camp or backpack in Glacier National Park, be prepared to share your smores with North America's most unique and elusive creature. —Rusty

1

MORE THAN MOUNTAINS AT FIFTY MOUNTAIN

I met Connor and his uncle, Denny, in a little mountain town in western Colorado, where Connor had a bike shop and his uncle had a grocery store. I'd stopped at the bike shop to see if they could recommend a bike for my wife Sarah's niece, who had a birthday coming up.

I ended up buying a nice bike from Connor, and I knew I was paying more than one from a big-box store would cost, but I didn't mind, as it was top quality. Besides, the story that came with it was priceless.

We all ended up getting lunch at Denny's small grocery store there and having a picnic down along the creek, where Connor told me the following story as his uncle listened, adding a few details here and there. I know it gave me pause, and I doubt if I'll ever go on this particular hike in Glacier National Park, at least not alone. —Rusty

Rusty, I'll never forget the day my Uncle Denny came to visit us, as it was literally a life-changing event—well, combined with some other life-changing events that happened along with it, that is. Denny's my favorite uncle, and his invitation to go hiking with him changed my life, hopefully for the better. But let me explain, as I know this sounds kind of dramatic.

I'd just graduated high school, and it was early July. I'd quit my summer job working as a server at a small restaurant in the little town of Hungry Horse, Montana, where I lived with my parents. I had plans to go to Montana State over in Bozeman that fall, where I was going to major in civil engineering. My dad was a civil engineer, and I guess I'd inherited some of his aptitude for it, as the university had given me a full scholarship.

I was chomping at the bit to get out on my own, especially since my dad and I had been butting heads for some time about most everything in general, and my latest shenanigan of quitting my job had really set him off. It seemed like I couldn't do anything right, and I was pretty much avoiding him, leaving the house in the evenings when he got home from work, mostly just riding my bike around or hanging out with friends.

Uncle Denny's my mom's brother and owned a small grocery store back in a little town in Kansas. He was on vacation, on his way to the Oregon coast, stopping to see us on the way and to spend a couple of days. He and I seemed to be on the same wavelength, in spite of the difference in our ages.

But that particular evening, sitting out on the back patio of my parents' house, I found out my mom and dad had been talking to him about my inability to stick with what I'd considered to be a pretty lowlife job, and it made me mad at them, as well as at him.

"Connor, I hear you're currently unemployed," my uncle said.

"It was a crappy job, Uncle Denny," I replied, irritated. "They paid minimum wage and expected me to do everything. Besides, the manager was a real jerk."

"How so?" Uncle Denny asked.

I'd been really enjoying hanging out with my uncle until then, as he treated me like an equal instead of a kid, but his question irritated me, and I really didn't want to talk about it. I'd already gotten a lot of flack from my parents about quitting, especially from my dad.

I answered, "He was highly critical. I couldn't do anything right. Plus he made me share my tips with the busboy."

"I thought that was pretty standard in the restaurant business," Denny replied. "But are you sure that wasn't just an excuse to quit?"

Now I was *really* getting irritated. In retrospect, I kind of had a chip on my shoulder at that point in my life. I wanted to be independent, yet it scared me at the same time. I was pretty nervous about going off to college, and yet I couldn't wait to be on my own.

And it seemed that my parents were going through some kind of stage in life where they just couldn't accept me for who I was. I have to laugh about it all these years later, as I was the one going through the stage, but at the time, I thought it was everyone else.

I answered, "I don't understand why me quitting a crappy job is such a big deal. I wish everyone would just let me enjoy my last summer before I have to go off on my own. Mom and Dad don't have to pay for my college. I got a full ride."

"And I'm very proud of you," Uncle Denny said. "They are, too. But won't you get bored all summer with nothing to do?"

I laughed. "With my imagination? I've never been bored in my life. It's only a couple of months until school starts. But what would be cool is if I could go with you to Oregon. That would get me out of here. You'd make me and my parents very happy."

Denny laughed. "You know, your mom and I drove up the Going to the Sun Road yesterday while you were over at your friend's. Glacier's sure a beautiful park. I've decided to spend my vacation here instead of going to the coast."

"Really?" I replied. "That's cool. We can go hiking together."

There was nothing I liked more than hiking in Glacier National Park. Even though it was in my back yard, I'd never got to do much there, other than a few day hikes, as my dad was always working and my mom wasn't much for hiking, as she was a landscape gardener and was outdoors all the time anyway. I'd mostly gone with my friends and their families.

"I was hoping you'd say that," Uncle Denny replied. "That's what I was getting at with you not working, that you might like to go out with me. Let's go into Kalispell and gear up."

Well, that really turned the conversation around, and it's also when I realized that my uncle was talking about backpacking, not just day hiking, 'cause you don't need to gear up to day hike.

To make a long story short, the next day, my uncle and I were standing at the Packer's Roost trailhead, the beginning of what was supposed to be a three night, four day backpacking loop in Glacier National Park.

If you ever want to take this hike (and you might not after reading my story), as you're driving up the Going to the Sun Road, you'll see an unpaved road to the left that leads to the Packer's Roost trailhead. This gravel road is very narrow and ends in a small clearing. It's used to trailer horses that pack supplies up to the Granite Park Chalet. The trail to Flattop Mountain, where we went, also starts there. The pack trail leads directly to the Granite Chalet, but we were going to take a very roundabout route that was much farther.

It was a hike lots of people did, nothing unusual at all about it, or so we thought. We had it all planned out, and when we got our backpacking permits at the visitor center at Apgar, the ranger also thought it would be a great trip.

He told us that the Fifty Mountain area was about as far away from civilization as you can get in Glacier. It was about 20 miles north of Logan Pass and about 10 south of Goat Haunt and was a true Glacier Park hiking adventure. Well, he was right about that, for sure, as we found out.

OK, so we would hike the first day to a campsite at Flattop Mountain, then hike to the Fifty Mountain camp on day number two, then on the third day, we'd head back south along a section of the Highline Trail to Granite Park. There's a backcountry chalet at Granite, but we'd camp at the nearby campground.

The last day we'd hike back down to the Going to the Sun Road, coming out at the Loop, where we'd hitch a ride back to the park town of Apgar. The Loop's this big switchback in the highway where there's a parking area. Lots of hikers hitched in the park, so we knew we'd get a ride. We'd call my mom to pick us up once we got to Apgar.

My uncle spared no expense in outfitting us, and I ended up with some nice gear. He even bought me a really expensive Gore-Tex jacket, which I still have.

Both my uncle and I were well-equipped with two cans of bear spray each, even though we were trying to pack light. We each carried one in a holster on our belts and a backup in a pocket on the outside of our packs. Where we were going, Fifty Mountain, had one of the greatest concentrations of grizzlies in the entire park, as well as black bears.

Fifty Mountain was famous for its bears, and I think that's actually why my uncle chose this route. Living in flatland Kansas, I think he was ready to see some wildlife and have a memorable vacation—which I'm happy to say he did, though it was maybe a bit too memorable.

OK, I was 18 and my uncle was in his 40s, but we were like best friends, we had so much in common. And after this trip, we had even more in common, because we'd both seen something few believe in, yet alone actually see.

And I'll say that Uncle Denny, who was divorced and had no kids, kind of became my surrogate dad after all this, and we're still very close. Don't get me wrong, I love my dad, but my uncle, like I said before, treated me like an equal, which was something my dad never did until I got older.

So, there we were, all geared up, lots of freeze-dried food and such, standing at the trailhead, ready to head out. We were both feeling a mixture of anticipation and nervousness, as this would be the first backpacking trip for both of us. My mom had dropped us off, and now we were the only ones there.

Or so we thought, for as we stood there, kind of fiddling with our packs and getting everything just right, here comes a woman who looked to be about my age, blonde hair and a pretty face, carrying a small daypack.

She smiled at us, not saying a word, then kept going right up the trail. We waited a minute, figuring her buddies would soon follow, but nobody did.

In retrospect, she gave me a chill—there's no other way to

describe it—yet I had no idea why. She seemed perfectly normal and had a pleasant demeanor.

"Not so good hiking in bear country alone like that," my uncle said, shaking his head. "The ranger said it wasn't even that great for parties of two, that four or five was the best."

"Maybe she's just going a short ways," I replied.

"Obviously just day hiking," my uncle replied.

With that, we started what would become one of the most memorable trips of my life—and even though this was a number of years ago, nothing's topped it yet, and I doubt if anything will.

Anyway, I've done some backpacking since then, though in Colorado, not Glacier, and I'll say that every trip starts the same—with pain. It takes awhile to get used to the weight on your back, no matter how well your pack fits, and on top of that, it also takes awhile for your body to get oxygenated. After awhile, though, you kind of get into a zen-like state and it becomes something that you almost enjoy.

Even though the trail followed McDonald Creek for a few miles, it was hot. It felt like it was at least 90 degrees, so we would stop occasionally and pour water over our heads. We finally crossed the creek and began the 2,200 foot climb to our camp.

We weren't in good enough shape for this kind of climb, but at least a big ridge blocked the sun, and it finally started cooling off as we slowly made our way up the switchbacks along Flattop Mountain.

Every once in awhile, we'd pass small waterfalls, and with the long views out across the valley, it started feeling like we were in some kind of wonderland. And once we topped out, the wildflowers everywhere added to the growing sense that we'd left our own world far behind.

It seemed like it took forever, but after a total of six miles, a lot of it up steep switchbacks, we reached the Flattop Mountain campsite. In retrospect, we should've picked something less ambitious, especially since we weren't in that great of shape.

I mean, I was active, riding my bike everywhere, so it didn't affect me as much as it did my uncle, even though working in a grocery store isn't exactly sedentary. But he was from the flatlands, and I think the altitude got to him, as he puffed a lot and had to stop every so often.

So, there we were, surrounded by high mountain peaks, a beautiful sunset making everything glow, including the bark of the numerous dead trees all around from some forest fire. The dead trees made it easier to see out, as all the needles were gone.

We were almost too exhausted to pitch our tents and eat dinner, but that done, we finally sat on some logs in the food-prep area to try to process where we were. What a difference from where we'd been just hours before!

I looked around, wondering where the woman we'd seen at the trailhead was. I knew there were other campsites nearby, but we couldn't see anyone, and it was as quiet as a church on a Saturday night.

From the looks of her small pack, I didn't think the woman could be camping—maybe she was a trail runner and had gone on to the Fifty Mountain camp, though that was another six miles, and maybe even on to Granite Park Chalet, another 11.5 past that. If so, she must be in really great shape, though for a trail runner, that wasn't a huge distance. But I did remember reading that the park discouraged people from trail running, as you were likely to startle a bear and get injured, or worse.

I wondered if she had a backcountry permit, as the park doesn't like to see people go out alone, but I guess they can't discriminate. If you're that brave (or some might say dumb), they have to give you a permit, I guess, though I'm not sure.

We pretty much collapsed into our tents, which we'd set up pretty close to each other, the lecture the ranger had given us about bears making us wary. As I lay there, drifting off, I remember thinking that we'd made it to our first camp and this would be our first night and how fast it would all go.

I then thought about going home and my dad and college and before I knew it, I'd drifted off and it was dawn. I opened my tent flap, and I could see the eastern sky taking on a pale blue, all the dead trees around our camp looking like tall black sentinels against the slowly changing colors. I'd slept like a rock.

I lay very still, and I could hear my uncle's breathing in his nearby tent, slow and methodical, and I knew he was still sleeping. It all felt very primal, being out there with nothing but a thin nylon tent for protection, surrounded by the wilds, kind of like early humans must have lived (without the nylon, of course).

But now I could hear a distant lone cry coming from far away. It had to be a wolf! Uncle Denny had told me he'd read about some backpacker watching a black wolf playing in the meadows not far from the campsites here.

"Uncle Denny, wake up!"

I wanted him to hear it, too.

I heard a muffled groan, then he said, "Too early."

The wolf howl had stopped, so I lay there, slowly waking, trying to figure out some weird dream I'd had about the blonde woman that I couldn't quite recall.

Now I could hear something in the bushes near my tent, and my first thought was of bears, so I rolled over and grabbed my bear spray. Whatever it was, it was large, nothing like a deer, but something that seemed to be slowly walking nearby, as if checking out our camp. I was suddenly scared. Even with bear spray, I wasn't sure I could deal with a bear.

The sound gradually went away, and as the sun rose, things started to warm up. I got up and got dressed, then crawled out of the tent. Looking around, I made my way to the cooking area, where I started some hot water on my little stove for coffee, my bear spray at my side.

Uncle Denny was still sleeping, and we only had six pretty level miles to go that day, so I decided to let him rest. If he felt as stiff and sore as I did, it was going to be a long day.

I decided it would be good to try to walk off some of my stiffness, so I got my mug of coffee and started slowly walking around camp, trying to loosen up. It was hard to walk because of the dead timber everywhere, so I started down the trail, thinking I'd go a short ways and then come right back.

The forest was shadowy, and as I walked, I started feeling tense, like maybe I should go back. Just as I turned around, I caught a glimpse of something in the shadows at the opposite edge of our camp.

There was something standing there, watching the tents! The only thing it could be was a bear, but if so, it wasn't a very big one, and the sun was backlighting what appeared to be blonde hair! I stopped and watched as it turned and disappeared into the trees, gone.

It was the woman we'd met at the trailhead! There was no doubt, her blonde hair shone in the sunlight, and she was the right size. But why would she spy on our camp like that?

I thought about following her and asking her what was up, but she'd disappeared into the thick forest, and like I mentioned, I felt uncomfortable.

Now back at camp, I knew Uncle Denny was still sleeping by the way he was snoring, and I decided to wake him. Even though we were now at a higher altitude and it was much cooler, it would still be better to hike before it got hotter, plus there was no sense in wasting the day away. I had to laugh as I made breakfast, as he was sleeping like the teenager and I was acting like the adult, cooking and getting him up and all.

We lounged around camp for awhile, eating freeze-dried scrambled eggs with bagels and drinking coffee, then finally got packed up and headed out.

I told him about the woman, and he seemed as puzzled by it as I was. We watched as we headed out, half-expecting to run into her, but we saw nary a sign of her or anyone else.

After hiking uphill for a short distance, we were soon in a huge meadow surrounded by dead trees, with incredible views in every direction and wildflowers everywhere under deep-blue skies. We were basically hiking across Flattop Mountain, and we could eventually see our destination, the Fifty Mountain Campground, in a large meadow across the valley. It was a fantastic day, and rugged Cathedral Peak stood high above us, making for some really photogenic scenes.

Suddenly, Uncle Denny grabbed my arm, stopping me, silently pointing to a small dot on a hill across from the meadow, with another even smaller dot near it.

"Grizzlies," he said excitedly, getting out his camera. "A sow and her cub."

"I hope you have a good telephoto," I replied.

I would've probably never even noticed them, as they blended into the landscape so well and were so distant, but knowing they were there made my heart stop for a minute.

"Oh Jeez," Uncle Denny said, his camera to his eye. "There's someone hiking right beneath them. I wonder if they even know the bears are up there."

"It's probably that woman we met at the trailhead," I said.

He replied, "It does look like her, and she appears to be alone."

He watched for awhile, then added, "She's gone. The bears didn't pay her any mind, even though she went right by them. Either she didn't see them or she wasn't afraid, but I know I don't want to hike near them like that. Our luck might not be as good."

We ended up taking a long detour around the bears, bush-whacking through deadfall, which was a big pain, but we finally got far enough away that we could get back on the trail without worry. I was glad to put them behind us, and I could tell Uncle Denny was relieved, also.

The irony was that we'd been more likely to run into bears on our detour than if we'd just stayed on the trail. I read later that grizzlies in Glacier don't seem to pay people on well-used trails much mind, as they're kind of habituated to it, and are more likely to get irritated when they see you in unexpected places.

We now started down a series of switchbacks, and the view ahead was incredible, looking out to the numerous rugged snowcapped peaks of the Continental Divide. We would soon be at the Fifty Mountain camp.

Fifty Mountain was called that because you could see 50 peaks from there. It's basically a huge alpine shelf that rests along the western side of the Continental Divide, and on the shelf is a huge meadow that's covered in bright yellow glacier lilies in the summer as if someone had planted a huge field of them. Bears love the lilies, accounting for why so many frequented the area.

We were soon at the campground, where we chose a small camp-site surrounded by logs to set up our tents. Most of the camps in Glacier have a central food prep area, making sure you don't cook near where you'll be sleeping and thereby attract bears.

After setting up our tents and sitting on the logs for awhile, drinking water with Gatorade powder in it, we headed for the prep area to start dinner, even though it wasn't that late. We were both starving, although we'd been snacking all day. Carrying a big pack up and down rough terrain does that to you.

After dinner, I walked around the campsites, half expecting to see the lone woman, but we were again the only ones there. Even early July can be sketchy for backpacking in Glacier, as the snow can still be deep. It had been a mild winter, so we weren't having any trouble with snowbanks and such, though we knew that could change on up the trail.

I was surprised to not see the woman at Fifty Mountain camp. It would be illegal for her to camp anywhere besides the designated areas—and what was she using for camping gear? Her pack had been too small to hold much, and the night had been cold. And I knew that if I were alone, I'd want to camp close to others in grizzly country—but of course, I wouldn't go up there alone in the first place.

It was getting on toward dusk, and my uncle and I sat on the logs around the cooking area, relaxing and enjoying the views. This second day had been much easier on us, primarily because we hadn't had to climb 2,200 feet up steep switchbacks. I was actually feeling kind of sad that tomorrow would be our last full day, and I could tell my uncle was feeling the same way.

Finally, he said, "Connor, I need your advice on something."

I was surprised. For him to ask my advice was a big compliment.

He continued, "Coming up here makes me realize how much I miss being out in the woods. There's nothing like this in Kansas, that's for sure. I'm thinking about selling my store and moving out here. It would also be nice to be closer to you guys."

I was surprised. "You'd miss those tornado sirens, Uncle Denny. They keep you on your toes."

He laughed. "I actually have a friend who wants to buy the store. I'm going to call him when we get back. Do you think that's a good idea?"

I laughed. "You have to ask?"

"And I'm going to buy a small van and trick it out for camping, you know, a bed, solar, that kind of thing. Maybe you and I can get out and see some country, though I'm not sure I can do much of this kind of thing, so we might end up doing more day hikes. I'm pretty sore."

I replied, "If it's any consolation, so am I. But what would you do to make a living?"

"I think I'll open one of those espresso drive-through shacks. Hungry Horse is a good place, lots of tourists. I'll hire someone to run it when I want to take off. You know, Connor, I don't need much to live on, and selling my little grocery store will give me a financial buffer."

I was silent, watching the sun go down over the mountains.

My uncle didn't know it, but he was in the process of changing my life, making me re-evaluate things I'd never even thought about before.

He was going to sell his store to come out here. He wasn't letting anything get in his way, and it seemed right to live like that. So why should I go study engineering when my heart wasn't in it? Just because I had an aptitude for it didn't mean it was what I wanted to do.

"I think you just helped me figure out why my dad and I aren't getting along," I said quietly.

Uncle Denny looked surprised. "How?"

"I think deep inside I resent him for pushing me to do what he thinks I should do. Just because he's an engineer doesn't mean I should be."

Uncle Denny looked thoughtful. Finally, he said, "Well, Connor, he wants you to have a good life, have a profession that will give you some security and enough money to live well. You can't really blame him for that."

"I know that, now," I replied. "But I've decided I'm not going to college, at least not right away. I want to do like you, be out in the wilds as much as I can. I need to figure out how to do that, 'cause that's what I want to do with my life."

"You could be a guide here in Glacier," Uncle Denny said. "Or anywhere you want, for that matter."

"Or I could help you run your espresso stand and we could go camping together. Would that work for you?"

"Your parents would probably hate me," he replied, smiling. "But sure, that would work just fine for me, at least for awhile, though it's not something you're going to want to do your whole life. Anyway, I'm going to have to hit the hay. I'm exhausted."

It was almost dark as my uncle crawled into his tent, and I knew from the light of his headlamp that he was reading. He'd brought a book along, something about Zen and motorcycles that he'd said was a classic, which meant it was written when he was young, I guess.

I sat there awhile in the near-dark, listening to some kind of owl hooting far away. It gave me a mournful feeling, and I suddenly missed my parents.

As I thought about what my uncle had said, how my dad just wanted what was best for me, I could feel something changing, a kind of softening inside, if you could call it that.

But I forgot all that when I again heard the howling—but this time it sounded odd, like something trying to imitate a wolf, not at all like the previous howl I'd heard.

To my surprise, I could now hear what sounded like a pack of coyotes in the distance, yipping and carrying on like crazy.

I was perplexed. I'd read that when reintroduced into Yellowstone, the wolves had pretty much killed or run off most of the coyotes. Were there big packs of coyotes here in Glacier, even though there were also wolves? I'd never really thought about it before, but maybe I could research it when I got home. It sounded like a sizable pack, for sure.

Now, one of the most incredible sights I've ever seen began to unfold as the full moon rose over the spine of the Rocky Mountains and Cathedral Peak, lighting up the meadows and making the trail look like a long brown snake through the glowing yellow glacier lilies. I wished I was a good photographer, as it was truly a once in a lifetime shot. I then noticed that long lenticular clouds were now moving in, a portent of bad weather.

And as I sat there, about ready to crawl into my tent, I could make out something coming up the trail towards our camp. I immediately felt chilled, thinking it had to be a grizzly, wondering where I'd put my bear spray.

Just as I was ready to alert my uncle, I could see it was small and walked upright like a human. It was the lone woman, coming our way. I wondered if she would stop or stay on the trail and bypass us.

But now I could see something on the trail behind her. I knew from its size it had to be a bear, and I called out to my uncle to come see. He quickly crawled from his tent, and we watched as it began to gain on her. She seemed totally unaware, not changing her pace any. Strangely enough, it, too, was walking upright, but it was no human with its broad shoulders and bulk.

"It looks like it's stalking her," Uncle Denny said with concern.

"Isn't there anything we can do?" I asked.

Just then, the woman, almost as if hearing us, turned and faced it. Instead of attacking, it stepped off the trail, quickly disappearing into the shadowy moonlit trees, as if afraid. She then turned back on the trail and disappeared into the distance, just as we heard another strange howl. It all seemed really odd.

"What do you make of that?" Uncle Denny asked.

"I don't know. It's weird. What was following her?" I asked.

"Whatever it was, it was big, Connor."

"It had to be a big grizzly. I read the park recently trapped one up in this area that weighed 1,000 pounds."

Uncle Denny shook his head. "I hope she's OK, and I hope it doesn't come up here."

We both sat in the moonlight on a log next to our tents. We were tired, yet neither of us wanted to crawl inside. It seemed like we were having the same thought, like we needed to be out where we could see. I felt that same chill I'd felt when the woman had passed us on the trail, and I was fighting the urge to flee.

"Connor, I feel really unsettled about all this. Something strange is going on."

"Agreed," I said. "Maybe we should pack up our camps and head back. There's enough moonlight to see, plus we have our headlamps."

"Do you think we're overreacting? Maybe because all this is new to us?" Uncle Denny asked.

I thought for awhile, then said, "No, not at all. You know, we need to trust our intuition. Dad always told me that. And my intuition says that we need to get out of here. Let's go back and find a campsite off the trail where we're hidden."

"Connor, I agree with you, but let's try to be stealthy about it. Hurry, pack up as quickly as you can, then we'll head back down the trail without using our lamps."

It didn't take long for us to get out of there, and I felt a black forbidding feeling the entire time, which didn't go away until we were a good couple of miles back down the trail.

We finally came to where we could see a small meadow back through the trees. After making sure we were out of sight of the trail, we again made camp.

That night, we took turns sleeping, Uncle Denny wanting me to keep reassuring him that we hadn't lost our minds. But after discussing the dark feeling we'd both had, I think we both came to a resolution—something strange was going on, and we needed to get back, to leave Glacier and return to safety. We both agreed it felt like our lives were at risk.

That dark feeling was worse when we rose the next morning to gloom and doom, or at least that's what the sky looked like, dark

clouds gathering from the west. But at least the night had been quiet
and I'd slept well, at least when I wasn't on watch, staring into the
bushes, listening for the slightest sound.

After breakfast and coffee, Uncle Denny said, "OK, time for a
reality check. Are you still feeling like you did last night? Should we
hike on out or turn around and try to make the best of what's left of
this trip? We can still go forward, if you want. We've lost a couple of
miles, but we can make them up."

I nodded with concern at the clouds overhead.

Uncle Denny replied, "When I checked the weather with the
ranger, he said a big storm was coming in, but we would have several
days before it hit. But it looks to me like it's coming in faster than they
predicted. We can go ahead and hike to Granite Park today, which is
12 miles from Fifty Mountain, spend the night there, then hike
another four to the highway, or we can keep hiking back, which
would be 12 miles total, minus the couple we hiked last night."

I thought for the longest time. This was supposed to be our epic
hike together, yet it would still be here in the future. I thought again
of the strange foreboding I'd felt the previous night.

Finally, I said, "Given what looks like a big storm coming in, I
think we should go back. If we go ahead, we'll have to cross the
Ahern Drift, and it could be treacherous this time of year."

Uncle Denny replied, "The ranger told me since it was a low snow
year, the Drift wasn't bad. He didn't think we'd need ice axes and
crampons. I was also hoping we could go up to the Sue Lake Overlook, which is a little out of our way but supposedly has incredible
views."

As we sat and talked, trying to make our decision, the winds
started picking up and the temperature began dropping, as if telling
us what we should do.

Finally, I said, "Uncle Denny, tell me why we're camped here
instead of back at our original camp last night. Did we both have the
same weird feelings at the same time from coincidence? Did we feed
off each other's fears?"

My uncle replied, "You're right, Connor. Something's not right, and even though we're feeling better about things this morning, we need to go back. This weather's too iffy, and at least the trail back is pretty easy. We'll be going downhill for the most part."

I stood and hoisted my pack on my shoulders. "We can come back another time."

We started back down the trail just as the winds started picking up, blowing straight in our faces. As we trudged along, I began to feel somewhat desultory, not really wanting to go back to my dad and the long summer ahead with no work and having to tell him I wasn't going to college. Maybe I could go back to Kansas with Uncle Denny and help him get things ready to move.

As the winds howled through the dead trees, we got more concerned about snags blowing over, so we upped our pace. I think we both felt we'd made the right decision and now just wanted to get back as soon as possible.

It took us several hours to hike back to the Flattop Mountain camp, where we then stopped for lunch, quickly throwing together some PBJ sandwiches. We didn't stay long, but before starting out again we put on our warm coats, hats, and gloves, as the temperature was still dropping.

We hadn't gone far when it began spitting snow. I was now worrying that we'd get caught in a blizzard and not be able to see the trail. I knew that Glacier could get deep snows any time of year, and even though we had warm coats, we weren't really relishing the thought of fighting a blizzard.

We upped our pace even more, Uncle Denny in the lead and me in the back, as he was the slowest. I knew the weakest link should set the pace when hiking, but we had no time to waste, and I knew I could help push my uncle along if he got tired.

Finally, the landscape seemed to slip out from under us, and I knew we'd reached the switchbacks. This was good news, for we would lose a lot of elevation, which would hopefully help moderate the weather. A good two inches of snow had now fallen, and I really wanted to get off the side of the mountain before it got deeper, making the trail more treacherous.

I could tell my uncle was tiring, so we stopped long enough for me to transfer some of his stuff into my pack, lightening his load. He protested, but when I told him we needed to keep up a good pace, he quit arguing. I think we were both beginning to feel like we were on the edge, especially if the snow got deeper, and the rate it was falling, we had little time left.

As we were stopped, snow swirling around us, I thought I heard the howling again in the distance behind us. It sounded mournful and even menacing, but I wasn't sure if it wasn't just the wind. In any case, it chilled me to the bone.

As we made our way down the narrow switchback trail, I was beginning to feel depleted, and all that seemed to exist anymore was the trail, the swirling snow, and the cloud bank that filled the valley below us.

We were finally at the bottom, and when I nearly ran over Uncle Denny, I knew we had to stop and do something to boost our energy levels. We'd gone at least eight miles and had another two or so to go, by my estimate, since we'd already walked out a couple the night before.

I knew we'd never make it out without stopping to replenish ourselves, even though we were now close to the trailhead, and we would probably have to walk the mile or so back to the highway, as it was unlikely that there would be anyone there. We needed to brew some hot tea and eat something, plus take a break.

I quickly pulled out my little stove and pan and set to brewing hot tea. My uncle sat on a rock, his back to the wind, and I used him as a windbreak for the stove. We were soon both drinking the tea and eating cookies, snow plastering our coats and legs.

Quickly putting our stuff away, we were quickly back on the trail. We both worried the storm would turn into a whiteout, making it impossible to even see where the trail was, though we did have the creek to one side. We just needed to get out.

I was again trailing behind my uncle when I heard something strange. The wind wasn't as severe as it had been on top of the mountain, but it was still moaning through the trees, and I at first thought that was what I was hearing. If you've ever hiked in a bad snowstorm, you know the snow kind of dampens the sound, and I thought at first that I was just hearing the wind pick up again.

But Uncle Denny heard it too, and he stopped, turning and putting his arm out for me to stop, saying, "Something's following us."

Now the howling began again, and it sounded like it was right behind us, just around a bend in the trail where we couldn't see it. I remember that instead of being afraid I felt confused—didn't bears have enough sense to find shelter in storms like this? Why would one be expending its energy to stalk us? Or did it even know we were ahead of it? And how could a bear howl like that? I figured it had to be a bear from the intensity of the sound, as no wolf could possibly howl that loud, but it didn't make sense.

And as these thoughts were going through my head, I was instinctively grabbing my bear spray and taking off the safety, and I could see my uncle was doing the same thing. And when I saw the look of horror and disbelief on his face, I knew I shouldn't turn to look, but I couldn't help myself, for I knew I had to face the danger head on.

There, coming up the trail behind us was a creature half again as tall as either of us and half-again as heavy, if not more. It was bulky and had thick hair from head to toe, hair that draped off its long arms in waves. It was dark brown, though almost entirely white from snow matted on it from the wind.

But the worst was that its face was almost human, though the nose was flatter, and its eyes—they glowed with hatred and anger and an intensity that made me want to close my own eyes in denial, knowing it had to be a dream. And it was almost upon us, and from the low guttural growl that came from its throat, I knew it was going to kill us.

I was frozen in place and couldn't move, and I remember thinking that this would be a really odd and painful way to die, then wondering if anyone would find our bodies. It seemed like time was standing still, and I was wondering why my uncle hadn't triggered his bear spray.

It was then that I was able to move, and as I raised my bear spray, finger on the trigger, I suddenly stopped, for the blond woman was there, right between me and this nightmarish creature, and I then knew it was going to be truly terrible to witness it mangling her instead of me, and where had she come from, anyway?

Upon seeing her, the creature seemed confused and stepped back for a moment, but then again came towards me as if to strike.

I pulled the trigger just as Uncle Denny pulled his. The creature stepped backwards, clutching at its eyes, bellowing in pain, for we'd both hit it straight on. It staggered backwards, then ran for the creek where it bent down and tried to wash its eyes.

"Quick, Connor, get out your other can! It's going to come back!"

I reached for the can of spray in the side pocket of my pack just as the creature stood, water draining from the matted hair on its face, still clutching at its eyes. Now the woman stood again between it and us, motioning for us to run while the creature again looked confused.

There was no way we were going to just leave her there to fend for herself, so Uncle Denny and I stood there, waiting.

Now the woman made a strange gesture at the creature, which looked even more confused. After some hesitation, looking like it was going to again come after us, it finally crossed the creek and climbed up the opposite bank, disappearing in the swirling snow.

And as we turned, we could see the woman was also gone.

I know we were both in shock, and we wanted nothing more than to run, but we worried about her. Where had she gone?

And now, the strangest feeling came over me, and as I stood looking at my uncle, both of us stunned by what had just happened, I could see from the look on his face that he was also confused and frightened. But now a woman's voice was telling me to go, go now, and don't look back, just get out!

I grabbed Uncle Denny's arm, turned him around, then told him to go, to run.

He did, and we both ran hard until we couldn't run any farther, our sides aching, and before long, we were back at the trailhead. It was snowing so hard we could barely even see one another, and we knew we had to get back to the Going to the Sun Road.

It was less than a mile on out, but it seemed much longer, and though we both tried our best to hurry, by the time we got to the pavement we were barely able to walk.

It was now almost dark, and with the blizzard, we knew our odds of getting a ride were slim to none, and there was no cell reception to call out, so we both began trudging down the road. At least it wasn't as cold, and as the big, wet snowflakes half blinded us, soaking our legs, we heard a howl far in the distance behind us, which made us walk even faster.

I don't know how long we'd walked, but it was pitch dark when a ranger stopped and gave us a ride. He took us to Apgar, where we were able to call my mom and dad, who came and got us.

Even though we weren't due out until the next day, they'd been worried, knowing a blizzard was hitting Glacier. I don't know who was happiest, them or us, but I suspect it was us.

Uncle Denny stayed a few more days, then went back to Kansas, saying he'd be back soon. But a week or so later, he called me and told me he'd changed his mind.

I wasn't surprised.

He said I was welcome to come out there and help him with his store, he'd guarantee me a job and place to stay, but he'd been thoroughly intimidated by what we'd seen and wanted nothing to do with Glacier at this point. In fact, he was trying to talk my mom and dad into moving out to Kansas, as it would cost a lot less to live there and he was sure they'd be able to find work.

In the meantime, I'd told my parents I was going to delay college for awhile, even though it would mean giving up my scholarship. I wanted to instead go spend the summer with my uncle, which I did, working for him there at his little grocery store.

It was great, and we both got into biking, taking long rides in the evenings around all the farm fields. That part of Kansas was really mellow, though it got hot and muggy, but I didn't miss the mountains one bit.

I had no idea what to do that fall, but Uncle Denny said I could stay on as long as I wanted, so I ended up spending the winter there. I was surprised when my mom and dad came out to visit and check it all out. They didn't like it enough to move there, but they did decide to move to Colorado, which wasn't all that far, and I ended up also moving there and getting a job in a bike shop.

I eventually opened my own shop in the small mountain town they'd moved to, and Uncle Denny went ahead and sold his store and moved there, too.

What made us all give up on Glacier, one of the most beautiful landscapes on the planet? It of course had to do with what my uncle and I saw there on the trail, but the final blow was when I showed him an article I'd found on the Internet about a young couple that had gone missing on Fifty Mile Mountain.

No one could figure out what had happened to them, as they'd been doing the same hike Uncle Denny and I had started on, but they'd just flat-out disappeared. After two months of intense search-and-rescue, no trace was ever found.

The article had a photo of the pair, and as I studied it, I wasn't sure what to think, for the woman looked exactly like the one we'd seen up there, the one who had basically saved us from certain death. Uncle Denny said nary a word when I showed it to him, but I could tell he was really upset.

All these years later, it still gives me the creeps, and I sometimes still feel anxious when out at night, though it's getting better. I still have no idea what we saw or why, but I do know I'll never go back, even though I sometimes miss the beauty of Glacier.

But we hike some here in the Colorado mountains, and for some reason, it feels much safer. Maybe it's because there aren't any grizzlies, but I really don't think that's the only reason. And even though there is plenty of wilderness here, Glacier's an even wilder place, and though everyone should go see it, I'm not so sure about hiking the backcountry. Like that ranger said, it's probably best to go in groups of four or five, if you go at all.

2

THE TRAIL OF THE CEDARS

I met Jill through my wife, Sarah. It was a friend of a friend kind of deal, and it took awhile to track Jill down, as she was a traveling nurse and moved around a lot.

The little bit I knew about what had happened to Jill sounded pretty authentic, and I was really interested in talking to her. When I finally caught up to her, she was in Helena, Montana. Since I wasn't all that far away at the time, down in Bozeman helping my friend with his fly-fishing business, I took a day and met up with her. I'd heard a number of pretty scary stories from Glacier, and it was nice to hear one that was more heart-warming. —Rusty

Rusty, they say you don't have many memories from when you were really young as your brain just isn't well-enough developed, but I beg to differ. I had something happen to me when I was little that I'll never forget, and even though I'm now nearly fifty, I still can't decide if it's a good or a bad memory—so I guess maybe it's both.

When I was seven, my parents took my brother and me to Glacier National Park. It was part of a three-week road trip across Idaho,

Montana, and Wyoming from our home in Salt Lake City. My parents had a small vintage 1961 Shasta canned-ham camper trailer, and they pulled it with their almost new Buick. What a sight—that nice beautiful sedan pulling an old beat-up trailer!

My dad had finished refurbishing the trailer on the inside, but hadn't yet completed the outside. I remember that we got turned away from a couple of nice campgrounds because we looked like gypsies, much to my mom's chagrin. Of course, now she laughs about it.

So, we went from Salt Lake up through the southern part of Idaho into Montana, straight up to Butte, then on over to Missoula and up to Kalispell. After visiting Glacier, we went on to Yellowstone and the Tetons, but that's another story.

Part of the reason for going to Glacier was to visit my grandfather and his new wife in the little town of Columbia Falls, which is the gateway to the park. My grandfather had moved there years before, working in a nearby lumber mill before he retired. My grandmother had passed away a good 10 years ago, and he'd finally remarried the spring before we went up there.

My parents were anxious to see him and meet his new wife. If I recall correctly, her name was Lilian, but everyone called her Lily. She was a bit younger than him and very pretty, and we could tell he felt like he'd made quite the catch from the way he talked about her.

Now, my grandpa wasn't what you'd call wealthy, but he was what you'd call well-set, which means he'd done well with what he had, with a good retirement and a nice paid-for property. He'd bought 10 acres just out of town and turned it into a parklike setting, with paths and grass and big trees and a huge flower garden. And best of all, he'd built his own house—a beautiful cedar place that really impressed me, as you didn't see many cedar houses in Utah.

So, even though I was only seven, I clearly recall that house and its grounds, and I also remember the big barbecue he and Lily had for us when we showed up—it was the first time I'd ever had deviled eggs.

Mom and Dad slept in the guest room, and my nine-year-old

brother Grady and I got our little Shasta trailer all to ourselves, parked there by the house under a big tree. We were pretty happy about that after being cramped up in it with my parents on the trip up there.

I think my parents were happy about it, too, especially since traveling with Grady was like listening to fingernails on a chalkboard, hour after hour—he's the most hyperactive person I've ever known. If then had been now, he'd probably be on meds for being ADD. At least he managed to channel it into an appropriate profession when he grew up—owning a busy restaurant, but that's also a different story.

We were going to stay there a week, so the first day was spent with the grownups sitting around talking while Grady and I played in the big yard, climbing trees and doing whatever kids that age do.

The next evening, we all went out to dinner at some exclusive restaurant in Kalispell, which was Lily's idea. I got the feeling nobody else was very interested, as my mom and dad were still tired from the trip, but Lily insisted.

She and Grandpa got all dressed up, making my mom feel self-conscious, as she hadn't brought anything that nice. I think the only reason they let us in was because they knew my grandpa.

I remember my mom talking that night to my dad, out by the trailer, as they checked on us, making sure we were in bed, saying she felt Lily was a bit of an extreme personality. She then made us all swear to never repeat that, and it became a sort of inside joke for Grady and me. We would use the word extreme every chance we got around my mom, which irritated her to no end. My mom was really good-natured, and we loved teasing her.

Anyway, I'm telling you all these details for two reasons—one, to show a little kid can remember things quite well, which will be important later on, and two, to show you what kind of a person Lily was.

OK, so there we were, in this beautiful setting near Glacier, where we were getting rested up and visited up. Now, Grandpa was my dad's dad, not my mom's, and my dad wanted to spend some quality time alone with him, but every time they'd be out in the yard talking or something, here would come Lily. She acted like she was afraid to leave my grandpa alone with anyone.

So, finally, my dad hatched a plan. He would take Grady and my grandpa fishing on the nearby Flathead River. He didn't figure Lily would want to go, especially since she seemed to be taking a dislike to Grady, who probably deserved it, to be fair, as he was good at driving everyone nuts.

My dad's plan worked, and they all headed out for the day, leaving me and my mom and Lily, who had decided to take us into the national park on a little tour. We were all planning on going to Glacier the following day anyway for a picnic, but Lily decided she'd give us a sneak preview, which was fine with my mom and me, though my mom made sure it would only be for a few hours, as she had no intention of getting stuck with her for very long. At this point, I could tell my mom was starting to feel about Lily like Lily felt about Grady.

We packed a lunch, grabbed our jackets, and all jumped into Lily's car. Things went well all the way to West Glacier, the site of the park's headquarters, where we stopped and got a day pass, then we went to the shore of Lake McDonald, which was stunningly beautiful.

By then, Mom had figured out that Lily's extreme personality also included her driving skills, and she'd decided she didn't want to go any farther, especially not up the narrow Going to the Sun Road, which she'd seen enough pictures of to know it wasn't a walk in the park. No way was she going to put our lives in Lily's hands, and she was adamant about it, though she tried to be nice by saying she loved the lake and wanted to spend the day there.

Lily wasn't happy, but my mom out-stubborned her. After walking along the shore for an hour or so, we had our picnic, then sat for awhile, me getting bored and Mom getting more frustrated. She wanted to go back to Grandpa's house, and I could tell she'd had enough of Lily, who did nothing but tell everyone how great she was and how she'd really made Grandpa's life better, making him get out and walk and all and eat right and dress better.

She made it sound like he was this sedentary sloth before she met him, but we knew better—someone maintained all those grounds around his house, and we knew it wasn't her.

I think Lily liked having a captive audience, and she kept saying it was too early to go home. So, finally, my mom, desperate to get away from her incessant talk, suggested we go hike this short trail she'd seen in the park brochure, something called the Trail of the Cedars. It was just up the highway a few miles, quick to get to, and an easy hike on a raised boardwalk through some big cedar trees.

Lily had no choice, since she'd said she was going to show us Glacier, and we were soon at the parking lot. According to a placard there, the trail was less than a mile long, and the old-growth trees were red cedar and western hemlock, and the Lake McDonald valley was the eastern edge of the maritime climate of the Pacific Northwest, the humidity allowing the red cedars to grow to heights of 100 feet. It was a land of giants that had escaped fire and avalanches for hundreds of years, a wonderland.

Well, a wonderland it truly was. Wide boardwalks meandered through the most amazing trees I'd ever seen, some with trunks wider than I was tall, their trunks covered with the greenest mosses and cradled in giant ferns. The placard said that some of the trees were more than 500 years old.

And what was even neater was what they called Avalanche Gorge that cut right through the middle of the walk. Its deep polished walls were filled with the rushing whitewater of Avalanche Creek, which came from Avalanche Lake, only a short hike on up a ways.

I can't remember if there was another placard there, but about midway around the Trail of the Cedars was a junction with the trail to the lake, which was about two miles one-way. The area was carved by a massive glacier tens of thousands of years ago, leaving a large bowl with huge mountains nearly all the way around it, the shallow lake in the center.

My mom and I really wanted to hike to the lake, but Lily said she wasn't prepared for such a long walk, as it would end up being around five miles total. We asked some people walking by, and they said it was an easy flat hike. My mom decided we were going, regardless, and asked Lily if she would mind waiting in the car. We could easily hike that in an hour, or maybe two at the most.

Lily was irritated, but she finally gave in and agreed to go with us, but not for long, as she needed to get back to the house, which was ironic, seeing how that's where my mom had wanted to go not all that long before.

So, off we went. Now, this is a really popular trail, partly because it's so close to Lake McDonald and so accessible, but also because it's easy. It follows along Avalanche Creek, which at this point is just a wide fast-moving creek, though it soon entered the deep gorge along the Trail of the Cedars.

Even though there were lots of people, it was a really nice hike, and the lake was beautiful, with towering peaks around it and several tall narrow waterfalls tumbling from a high ridge, one called Monument Falls. And the Little Matterhorn, high above the basin, was quite impressive. I remember it all clearly, as it was the most beautiful thing I'd ever seen—there was nothing like that around Salt Lake, though the Wasatch are impressive in their own right.

I think even Lily was enjoying herself, but when someone said they'd seen a black bear nearby, she decided she wanted to go back. Mom and I wanted to stay longer, but we started back, Lily in the lead.

Now, what happened next I don't remember, which is ironic, as you would think of everything, this would be something I'd never forget. But one minute I was standing at the edge of the creek, and the next I was in it.

My mom said she didn't see what happened, but Lily said she saw me step on a rock that was loose and that flipped me into the water. The next thing I knew, I was being buffeted against rocks, tossed along in the water like a rag doll, stunned.

The water carried me along faster than one can run, and my mom and Lily soon lost sight of me, even though they were trying to follow along the bank, yelling and screaming, which alerted others, including a ranger.

I've since learned that more people die in Glacier in water accidents than from any other reason. The snow and glacial meltwater is cold, and the lakes never warm up above 45 to 55°F, creating the potential for quick hypothermia.

As I careened down the swift waters of Avalanche Creek, I recall worrying that I would soon be in the gorge, where the steep slick walls would make rescue impossible.

I was soon struggling to breathe, and I'd been slammed against enough rocks that I knew it was only a matter of minutes before I would pass out. I remember thinking of Grady and wondering how his life would be without his little sister. My last thought was of my mom.

I don't know how long I was out, but I remember waking to the strange sensation of being held against something warm and hairy that smelled like a wet dog. At that point, I didn't even know who or where I was, but I knew someone was carrying me.

I immediately started coughing up water and moaning, and whoever was holding me now held me upside down until I started choking, then again pulled me up against them, trying to warm me up.

As I gradually came to my senses, I looked up into the biggest yellow eyes I've ever seen. They were framed by a huge face all covered with dark red hair. I remember thinking it was a man who badly needed a shave, but then I realized the nose was all wrong, kind of big, yet flat, and I gradually became aware that what was holding me was no human. I was too out of it to care or even want to understand what was going on. I just wanted to go to sleep, so I drifted off.

Now the big man was shaking me, making me stay awake, and this made me resentful. I asked him why I couldn't just sleep, but he shook his head, trying now to get me to stand on my own.

I looked again into those eyes, which seemed to radiate a sense of compassion and worry, and I gradually began to remember what had happened, and I knew this creature had rescued me from the water. And as I stood, I could now see it better, and I understood then that it wasn't human, but was a soaking mass of wet hair and hugeness.

Now, above the sound of the nearby rushing creek, I could barely hear people yelling, coming my way, and the creature slowly turned to go, first patting me on the head with what seemed like affection. Its hands were huge and leathery, with no hair on the palms.

I should have been afraid, as this thing towered over me, but instead I felt a surge of appreciation. This thing, whatever it was, had saved my life. And as it turned to go, I reached out and grabbed it by the arm—I remember thinking how big and thick its arm was. It turned back to me in surprise, and I squeezed its arm, too weak to do anything more.

It smiled and was gone.

Now people were nearby, yelling, and I tried to yell back, but ended up coughing and collapsing. Before I knew it, my mom was there, crying, along with the ranger and several others, and they picked me up and carried me down the trail.

But here's the deal. When they got me back to Lily's car, she didn't want to let me ride in it because I was wet and smelled funny. My mom and I were actually taken to the hospital by the ranger, while Lily went on home. She later made what felt like a token call to see how I was doing, and though my dad and grandpa came to the hospital, along with Grady, Lily didn't come. I remember that Grady was white as a sheet.

I spent the night in the hospital, then was released the next day, sore and exhausted. No serious harm was done other than some bruised ribs that bothered me for the rest of our trip, but gradually healed.

The funniest thing about it all was the way I smelled. You'd think after being in the water for as long as I was I would smell nice and clean, but everyone was aghast at how I smelled like a wet dog. The hospital people cleaned me up, and my mom finally decided the smell was from all the mosses in the water, though that really didn't make sense, as I hadn't even seen any moss.

Once I was back, we managed to make the most of the few days left, driving the Going to the Sun Road and doing some sightseeing, but my dad insisted on taking our car, and Lily always came up with an excuse not to go, even though my grandpa would come along.

My mom told me later she thought Lily felt guilty about the way she'd treated me, but I wasn't so sure about that, thinking she was just being Lily.

Our last afternoon there, we again had a barbecue in the big yard, and the talk went to what had happened that day when I fell into the water. I had told Grady about what I'd seen, and he'd believed me implicitly, saying I'd been rescued by a Bigfoot. The whole thing kind of scared me, in retrospect.

So, I decided to tell everyone the whole story. Afterwards, nobody said a word, except Lily, who said I had to have imagined the whole thing. But my grandpa was silent for awhile, then finally said that he'd heard of a number of Bigfoot accounts by ranchers in the Flathead Valley and also some from the Blackfeet Reservation on the other side of the park.

But what got me was when he said that he himself once saw a huge, dark figure peering out from behind the big trees on the Trail of the Cedars. He laughed, saying he hadn't lingered to get a better look, as he'd been scared. This made me feel better, though Lily just rolled her eyes.

After the barbecue was over, it was getting on toward late afternoon, and my grandpa came over to where I was sitting on a stump and asked, "Jill, do you feel good enough to go back out where they found you? I think it would be a good thing before you go, you know, to give you some closure."

I wasn't sure what closure was, but I said that yes, I would like to go. I wanted my grandpa to see the thing that had saved me.

Well, my mom and dad and even Grady wanted to go along, so we were soon on our way to the Trail of the Cedars. Lily didn't want to go, of course.

I was still sore, so my grandpa and dad took turns carrying me on their shoulders. My mom knew exactly where to go, as she'd been the one who'd found me, and before long, we were standing next to the creek, though my dad made sure we didn't get close, not that any of us would've anyway.

Now my mom started crying, and my dad held her close, Grady also holding her hand. My grandpa asked, "Jill, do you feel like crying, too? If so, it's OK. This is what closure means. You revisit something and get out your feelings so you can move forward."

"I'm fine, Grandpa," I replied. "I just wish the hairy man would come out and let us see him. I don't think anyone believes me, except Grady."

"Oh, I believe you," Grandpa said. He'd asked Grady to carry a small daypack for him, and he now opened it, taking out a bag of apples and some carrots.

"We'll leave these as a thank-you gift," he said, then took a rock from his pocket and placed it next to the apples. On it Grady had painted the word, "Love."

As we all stood there, I suddenly felt as if something was watching, and I looked into the dark forest of old-growth cedars, but saw nothing. But I somehow knew the creature was there.

Grady now said, "I'm getting kind of creeped out. Can we go now?"

My dad laughed, and we all started back down the trail, me back up on my grandpa's shoulders. I turned and looked back, and over the roaring of the creek, I thought I heard something—it sounded like people yelling, looking for me. I felt really strange and wanted to cry, but couldn't, and the sound soon receded back into the roaring of Avalanche Creek.

We said our goodbyes the next day, and I remember sleeping most of the way to Missoula, propped up on pillows in the back seat because my ribs hurt.

I remember my mom and dad discussing Lily on the way back, and my dad saying that my grandpa was no fool and would eventually figure it out.

We all loved Yellowstone, but my parents didn't let me out of their sight for one minute, nor Grady, for that matter. But there was no need to. I wasn't going anywhere. I was too sore, plus I was still recovering from the scare of my life.

Grady told me years later that he'd been so unnerved by my story he was afraid to go anywhere in the woods alone for some time afterwards, even though he knew the Bigfoot had saved my life.

So, we finally got back home, and life went on much as it had been, nothing really new, except for the day my grandpa called and said he was coming for a visit. I could tell my mom was conflicted, as she wanted him to come, but she didn't want to have to entertain Lily.

But when he told her he and Lily had split up, she actually started dancing around. It was pretty funny, and Grady and I both started doing the same kind of little jig, everyone laughing as we sang a little chant with only one word—*extreme.*

After that, for some time, we'd do that little jig for no reason at all, even over little things like mom making deviled eggs. It always made her laugh.

So, when Grandpa showed up, we got the story about Lily, though there wasn't much to tell. Apparently, our trip had started the process of him opening his eyes, and he'd finally got tired of her telling him what to do all the time. They'd only been divorced a month, and she was already dating someone new.

Grandpa seemed much happier, and he asked me to tell him my Bigfoot story several times after that, saying it was quite the deal, and I knew he believed me. And when he was ready to go back home, he handed me a small plastic bag with something dark in it.

"What's this?" I asked.

"Jill," he replied, "When we went to visit you at the hospital, they gave us your wet clothes to take home. This was stuck to your jacket. I was going to give it to you before you left, but forgot. I thought you might like it as a keepsake."

I opened the baggie to see it had a bunch of long thick course hair, hair that still smelled faintly like a wet dog. I smiled, thanking him, thinking I had the best grandfather in the world.

3

DECEPTION ON MARIAS PASS

I met Ryan in a little Colorado mountain town where Sarah and I had gone to visit a friend. Since there was an art fair in the park, Sarah wanted to look around, so we stopped and spent some time looking at everyone's booths.

When I came to Ryan's tent, I was surprised at the quality of his watercolors, for they were more like something you'd see in an expensive gallery. His prices were reasonable, and his work was selling fast.

He had a number of pictures that looked like Glacier National Park, so we got to talking about them, as Glacier's always been one of my favorite parks. He had one of a mountain I'd never heard of called Dusty Star Mountain, and as we talked, he hinted that he'd seen something near there he'd found rather disturbing. I finally got him to tell me more after the show ended and Sarah and I helped him take down his tent. I will say, I have to agree with him—his story was indeed disturbing. —Rusty

My name's Ryan, and I have two Siamese cats, Meowlie and Growlie. Yes, I know they're dumb names, but my son named them, and even though I kept saying I was going to change them to something better, the names stuck.

I mean, they're Siamese, after all, and deserve names of distinction, but oh well. The cats are brothers, from the same litter, and I got them as kittens in a weak moment from Petco, where the local shelter had them on display for adoption. My son was involved, is all I can say.

I live in Spokane, Washington, and my cats now stay home when I go out, but this particular time they came with me. It was an experience that I don't care to repeat, and I'm sure they don't, either. I could say it was a night we'll never forget, but that somehow sounds cliche and doesn't begin to capture it. My two cat boys are both getting old now and prefer lazing around the house, and to be honest, I kind of do, too.

But this particular time I had big plans, and they were part of them. I was thinking about selling my house and hitting the road for a few years, traveling and seeing the country, doing watercolor painting and seeing if I could make a living at it. I had no intention of giving my cats away—I would take them along. I'd read about other people who traveled with cats, and it didn't seem like a big deal.

I had visions like on some social media site—me painting by some beautiful alpine lake, the cats lounging nearby on their leads, taking them for walks, sitting out watching the stars, that kind of thing. I would go to an occasional art fair to sell my paintings, which would make me enough to live on.

Was this a pipe dream? Maybe, but I'd been painting since I was a kid, and I was actually pretty good. I did mostly landscapes, and my specialty was lots of color, and I'd even do occasional animals and wildlife. I had actually sold a number of my paintings at shows, so I thought I was being well-grounded, and it was a lifelong dream, not something I'd just hatched up.

I didn't make all that much as a handyman anyway, so I knew I could survive on occasional sales, as I was used to being frugal. My wife had left years before, and my two kids were grown and on their own, so all I had was the cats and myself to look after. It seemed doable and even pretty simple, so why not?

I won't go into the virtues of Siamese because there are few. I love

Meowlie and Growlie, but they can be stubborn and independent and off in their own worlds—but wait, that describes most cats, doesn't it, and actually even a lot of people. But they always atone for their bad behavior at the end of the day when they come and snuggle up next to me in bed, purring like they love me to no end, though I know that, being cats, they're really just waiting for me to move so they can claim my pillow. I will say that Siamese are exceptionally smart, which ended up being a good thing this time.

I'm kind of joking, because we're all attached to each other, but I really think none of this would've happened if they hadn't been along. Bear with me, and I'll get there, but you have to know the backstory, so to speak.

I'd saved my pennies until I could get a nice camper for my pickup, which is a Toyota Tundra. Now, if you know much about the newer Tundras, you'll know that they made the bed's side rails taller than on American pickups, and most campers won't seat into the pickup's bed like they should. Campers have a narrow bottom part that's designed to sit down into the bed, then they flare out to provide more room inside.

So, I'd bought a used Lance camper, and when I put it on my Tundra, I had to build up the height of the pickup bed so the camper wasn't balanced on the side rails but was actually seated down into the bed. I don't know if I'm explaining this very well, but it becomes important later.

So, I put several pieces of plywood under the camper to raise the bed up, not really a big deal at all. The problem was, I bought the camper a year before I actually took off, and that was plenty of time for water to run down beneath it and start rotting the plywood, which I should've sealed, but didn't. I didn't realize it, but the rot had gone into the floor of the camper, as well as the sides where the tie-downs were. The whole thing was ready to fall apart. More on that later.

OK, I hadn't put my house up for sale yet, as I felt I needed to do a trial run before doing anything that permanent. I had talked to a real-estate agent, and she'd given me a sales number that was way more than I'd expected, so I was pretty excited. It was just a small bungalow in an older neighborhood, though I had fixed it up.

I mean, I could live for a decade or more on what she'd quoted me, as long as I lived in my camper, and if I could sell paintings, I could maybe even just stash it all in the bank as a backup fund and not even use it at all. It was beginning to look like this new life was not only possible, but wouldn't even be that hard to implement.

My ex was concerned, saying things like, where will you go when you're old or if you get sick—but that's mostly why we'd broken up. She and I looked at things from opposite perspectives, though we were still friends.

Anyway, Spokane's not that far from Glacier National Park, and I wanted to go someplace epic to start to my experiment. I'd been there years before, and I remembered it being a really stunning landscape, a place where I would never run out of things to paint, and it was such a popular park I knew people would buy paintings of it. I could also go around to some of the galleries and shops in nearby towns and see if I could get some accounts going.

So, I got all ready to go, getting food and water and making sure my truck was all serviced and that kind of thing. My daughter offered to take care of the cats, as she lived nearby, but I wanted to take them, as that was part of the whole reason for going, to see if this would work.

They would ride in their carriers in the camper, and I'd stop every couple of hours and let them run around inside for a bit. I really didn't think they'd be much trouble, and I was generally right—until later, that is.

Well, the big day dawned, and I can't tell you how excited I was. It was July and getting hot in Spokane, and I was ready for the cool mountains of Montana. I had my painting supplies, food and water, and everything we needed, and as I loaded the cats and locked the house, I was walking on air. I knew my life was going to change in a big way, and I was ready for it, or so I thought, anyway.

I got on the freeway headed east, at first feeling kind of nervous, but as the miles rolled on, I got more excited. I stopped every hour or so to check on the cats, and they were being so good I decided to let them out of their carriers.

They could get on the upper bunk and be more comfortable, as well as see me through the back window in my pickup, and they seemed much happier.

So, on we went, soon arriving in Missoula, then on to Kalispell and Glacier. I was going to spend two weeks, and I had high hopes of making some really nice watercolors.

Now, at that point in time, Glacier in July was a zoo. I haven't been back for awhile, but I would guess it's still that way, if not worse. Every pullover, every parking lot, every campground was full.

I hadn't anticipated that, and I knew I was going to have problems finding a camp spot, so after talking to a ranger, I decided to just go to the east side of the park for the day, places like St. Mary Lake and Many Glacier, where it wasn't quite as busy. Some of the campgrounds there are first come first served, so I hoped to maybe get lucky and snag a spot.

I was soon driving over the Going to the Sun Road, and if my camper had been any taller I wouldn't have been able to take it, as the road has restrictions. It was scary, as it's narrow, but I was soon on top of Logan Pass and then on down the other side to St. Mary.

Well, that side of the park was just as crazy, and none of the campgrounds anywhere had any openings. I went south towards the Two Medicine area, with no luck, so headed for East Glacier, which is on the Blackfeet Reservation.

No luck there, so I decided to go out of the park and just find a boondocking spot in the timber. I was exhausted and tired and didn't want to deal with anything more, just go to bed. Besides, I wanted to spend some time with the cats and make sure they were doing OK.

I don't know how familiar you are with Glacier, but Highway 2 skirts the south side of the park and goes over what's called Marias Pass. The railroad runs along there, and it's a fairly gentle pass, with Lewis and Clark National Forest on the side of the road opposite Glacier, as well as the Bob Marshall and Great Bear wildernesses.

The road goes through some really rugged territory, but it's a good way to bypass all the craziness of the park.

Well, it was almost dark, and even though the days are long that far north in the summer, once I topped over the pass, I knew I had to stop. I pulled off on a forestry road and went back a ways. As soon as I found a place where I could pull off in the trees, I stopped.

I have to admit that from the git-go, I was pretty spooked, and now knowing myself a little better, if I felt that way again, I would just turn around and get out of there.

But at the time, I was really tired and also worried about the cats and not wanting to subject them to any more travel on their first day out. What they ended up being subjected to later that night was definitely much worse than a few more hours of driving would've been, for sure.

I was basically parked under a big canopy of tall old-growth trees, the kind with big trunks with moss on them and so tall you have to practically fall over backwards to see the tops.

I recall standing there for a moment after I got out of the cab, looking up, noting a few stars were coming out, and feeling like I was the last person on the planet, it was so quiet. I had the urge to get right back in and take off, and I should've listened to my intuition.

The place felt really wild. I've been in lots of wilderness, as I used to backpack in my younger days, but this felt different. I really can't explain it, except to say it almost had a feeling of uncertainty to it, and it made me want to get into my camper right away, whereas normally I would've made a cup of tea and watched the stars come out, that kind of thing.

The cats seemed stressed, and I was careful to reassure them, giving them some of their favorite cat treats. They finally came and wanted on my lap, which is kind of hard to do with two of them, but I tried, petting them and holding them until they started purring.

I then made myself a sandwich and sat there in the dark, not wanting to turn on my inside lights. For some reason, I didn't want to be visible, as if there was someone outside watching, though I didn't actually think there was at that point, or I would've just left. But I felt unsettled.

I decided to just go to bed, feeling that my uncertainty was from being tired. I was very happy I'd chosen a pickup camper as a rig and not something I'd have to set up, like a pop-up trailer. I just didn't want to be outside in the dark.

For some reason, I decided to sleep on the bench seat instead of in the overhead bed. The bed seemed claustrophobic and like I wouldn't be able to get out fast enough if I needed to. Now, I'd camped in my rig before, going up to Priest Lake near Spokane, and I hadn't had a bit of trouble like that. But for some reason, I wanted to be down low where I could get out the door as fast as possible.

If I hadn't been so tired, I think I would've put all these strange feelings together and realized there was possibly something wrong there, something going on that I needed to just get away from, whether it was just my imagination or something real. Instead, I wanted to go to sleep and get some rest.

I basically passed out, and I don't know how long I'd been sleeping when something woke me—a deep rumble from the distance. I at first thought it was thunder, but it was continuous, and I finally woke up enough to realize it was a train coming over the pass. I slipped back asleep, half recalling some strange dream I'd been having where I was worried about something rotting in my little camper fridge and wondering how to deal with it.

I woke again, not sure how much later, to the sound of the wind whispering in the tall trees all around. I'm not sure what they were— larches, maybe Douglas fir—but they were tall, and when I roused myself enough to lean on my elbow so I could see out the window, I could see them against the starry sky, bending and dancing in the wind. I remember thinking I probably wasn't in such a good camp spot, should one come down, but I was so tired I tried to go back to sleep, the cats curled up next to me.

I began to toss and turn, unable to really get back to sleep, kind of half-dreaming about a tree falling on the camper. Next thing I recall was the cats both trying to get down into my sleeping bag, something they'd never done before. I knew they were cold, so I tried to accommodate them, though I was sure they'd get squished. Later, in retrospect, I knew it hadn't been that cold and they were scared.

I must've finally gone back to sleep, because the next thing I remember is dreaming that the cats were having a big fight. They're brothers and get along great, so this puzzled me, and when I woke, I realized they weren't fighting, but were sitting on top of me, looking out the window and yowling.

This was not something I'd ever heard them do, make this yowling sound, and it made me think there was something outside. I again looked out the window, but saw nothing, but I did note the wind was getting worse. Maybe it was time to get up and drive on, even though I was still tired, not having slept all that well.

But I was suddenly wide awake as something hit the side of the camper! Both cats bolted for the upper bed, where they could get back into the far corners, away from any windows. I guess they're smarter than me, because my inclination wasn't to hide, but to instead look out the window. Bad mistake.

I could see something standing next to the camper, and even though it was still dark outside, I could tell by its outline that it was huge. My first thought was that it was a bear, and my second thought was to wonder how I could get out and around to the cab so I could take off. And why would a bear hit the side of my camper? Had it been a branch falling?

The wind had really picked up, and even without the bear, I knew I needed to get out and away from the trees. I would be safer if I camped by the side of the highway until daylight, out in the open. I needed to somehow get into the cab, but there was no way I was going out there with a bear around.

My camper had a window that opened between it and the cab, and the last time I'd tried to crawl through it as an experiment, I'd nearly gotten stuck. But it now occurred to me that I really needed to crawl into the cab and drive away, sketchy as that would be.

I'd hung my keys on a hook above the couch, so I grabbed those, slipped on my boots, made sure the camper door was locked and the windows closed, then made my way to the window. I stopped, now thinking it would be a good idea to crate the cats in case something happened, so I reached up trying to catch them, but they were both in the far corner of the upper bunk, so I had to climb up there.

I managed to grab them both, then slide back down, and as I did, something again slapped against the camper. At that point, both cats started clawing me to get away, terrified. I managed to hang onto one, and since it was dark I wasn't sure which it was, but I got him into his crate, then went for the second.

Once I had them both in their carriers, I started to put them on the upper bunk so they would feel more secure, but I suddenly had second thoughts. I would push them through the window, and then they'd be in the cab with me and safer.

I managed to get the window open and push each carrier into the cab, then I crawled my way in, barely fitting through, at one point thinking I wouldn't make it, and so much for my favorite treat of ice-cream sandwiches. It takes a lot longer to tell this than it actually took to do it, as I was moving as fast as I've ever done in my entire life.

Once in the cab, I locked the back window, then put the keys in the ignition. I'd parked so I didn't have to turn around to pull out, which I always did when camping as a safety measure, as one never knows when they might need to get out in a hurry, though I'd always thought it would be a fire or something like that.

Now, from nowhere, just as I was ready to start the truck, a most curious thought came to me. I was tired, it was still dark, and why in heck would I want to just drive away and find a new place when I had no idea where to go? Why not just climb back into the camper and get some sleep, then in the morning, I could sit under the big trees and drink a cup of coffee, relaxed and well-rested?

There was nothing out there, it was just the wind, and it had already started to die down some. By morning it would be a nice blue-sky kind of day, and I could enjoy being in the shady timber. And what about all the wildflowers? I could enjoy them all around me, glacier lilies and lupine and even beargrass.

I relaxed, thinking staying was a good idea, wondering how I'd gotten myself so worked up. Then it occurred to me that there were no wildflowers here. If there were, I would've seen them when I drove in, as it wasn't yet dark. And beargrass and glacier lilies? I wasn't much of a botanist, but I did know that those plants were more high-altitude meadow plants, not ones that would grow here in the deep forest.

Now a new thought came to me. Just down the road was a really nice small lake, one full of all kinds of fish, and if I stayed, I could go fishing in the morning and have some fresh cut-throat trout for breakfast.

Well, I'm no fisherman, and I sure couldn't catch fish without a rod and reel, even if I were. And were cut-throat trout lake fish? I'd always thought they lived more in streams. And how did I know there was a lake?

Well, what about hiking? Just beyond the lake was a nice trail that led to the top of a nearby mountain where one could see all the majestic peaks over in the national park, as well as back into the Bob Marshall Wilderness. It was spectacular, something one shouldn't miss, especially being so close.

I wasn't going hiking, I told myself. There was no way I'd leave Meowlie and Growlie alone in the camper. Maybe at a campground where there were other people to keep an eye out, but not out here, where I could potentially come back to find my rig stolen or worse.

I shook myself awake, realizing I was dozing off, the key still in the ignition and ready to go. It seemed like I'd somehow been arguing with myself, and yet one part of me had the facts all confused, things like glacier lilies and trout in the wrong place and stuff like that.

The cats had settled down and were crouched in their carriers, quiet, but now, from nowhere, one of them let out the deepest throat-iest growl, a sound I've never heard them make before or since.

I now had another thought—this one more unsettling than the previous thoughts of flowers, fishing, and hiking—the thought that I was about to die. And as I looked out in front of me, I knew I was no longer dreaming, and what I saw was something I could never describe to anyone else, since I didn't believe it myself. Later, when I did try, I realized that the majority of what I saw that night was in my mind's eye, because it was too dark to actually see anything. And my mind's eye saw something truly terrifying.

All I could make out was what looked like large eyes glowing in the dark like two beams from flashlights, and at first I thought that's exactly what they were, two hikers standing in front of my truck. It finally dawned on me that what I was seeing were eyes, somehow shining from their own power.

Now the other cat was screaming, and I mean literally screaming. These darn Siamese couldn't see out of their carriers—how did they know something was there? They somehow knew, and their cries galvanized me from dreamland into action.

I started the truck and hit the accelerator, peeling out and nearly hitting whatever was in front of me, which jumped back and let out a scream that made the truck shake. And just as it screamed, which was the most ungodly sound I've ever heard, something hit my camper from the side, something hard.

I thought a tree had fallen on it, but later, when I went back to get it, there was no tree. Whatever it was, it hit just as I was making a sharp turn onto the forest road, and between whatever hit it, the wind, and the truck turning, it all combined to make my camper tumble right off the side of my truck bed, the rotted floor and walls unable to hold it to the tie-downs.

Thinking back, I should've heard it crash, but there was no sound at all. I think that was because the winds were howling by then, and my ears were also ringing from the scream, and I was also beginning to think none of it was even real, even though I saw it lying on its side as I drove away, my taillights illuminating it.

I was soon back on the highway, heading down the pass for West Glacier and eventually, Columbia Falls. Once at West Glacier, I pulled over and surveyed the damage. My truck was fine, except for a long scratch on the side where the camper must've scraped as it fell. The tie-downs were flapping in the wind, so I unbolted them and put them in the truck.

It was dawn when I got to Columbia Falls, where I pulled into a little roadside motel. The manager was awake and said they had only one empty room, and I took it, not even realizing I was still in my longjohns. I unloaded the cats and found an old cardboard box behind the motel and set up a litter box using dirt from their planter. I crawled into bed and slept for hours, finally waking around 10 a.m., the cats wanting their breakfast.

There was a Dollar-type store nearby, so I went in and got some cat food, as well as some sweat pants. After grabbing breakfast at a drive-through, I went back to the motel, fed the cats, changed out of my longjohns, then called a wrecker. I needed to get back up on Marias Pass and gather my stuff before someone else came by, as well as try to recover my camper.

The motel manager was a really nice gal, and after I explained to her that my camper had been hit by a tree, she said it was OK to leave the cats in the room while I went back up the pass. It was nice and cool inside, and I knew they'd be much better off there sleeping. They both seemed kind of frazzled, like I know I felt.

I was soon following the wrecker, and once on the pass, we headed down the forest road to the camper. When we got there, I was shocked to see it had been righted, no longer on its side. What was strong enough to lift a 1,000 lb. plus camper?

I unlocked the door and looked around, and everything seemed to still be there, though it was all in chaos, as the cupboard doors had all come open. And the outside wasn't even that banged up. Some of the fiberglass siding was smashed up, but it looked like it could be repaired. But where the tie-downs had been was all pulled out, and the floor was messed up.

The wrecker guy managed to winch it back on my truck, and he ran several cables across the top and secured it on so I could get it home.

To make what's become a long story a little shorter, I went back and got the cats, had lunch, and headed back for Spokane, getting in late that night, totally exhausted.

I had a couple of friends help me unload the camper the next day at a friend's repair place, and he actually ended up buying it from me as is. After what I'd been through, I had no desire to ever camp in it again. He got a real bargain, and I got rid of it.

But I knew I could never get rid of the memory. I had no idea what I'd seen, and I was still puzzled by the way I'd argued with myself, trying to get myself to stay. It just didn't make sense.

After talking to my kids about it, they both said something was trying to control my mind, and that this something probably didn't have my best interests in mind.

Well, the story should end here, but it doesn't, unfortunately—or maybe it's a good thing, because I finally did figure it all out, or so I think.

After all this happened, even though I was back in Spokane, I kept having the thought that I should go back—and take the cats with me. I could go over there and get a motel room, or I could even sleep in my truck.

I kept seeing myself walking the cats on leashes around that beautiful lake with wildflowers everywhere. It was the most comforting feeling, and it made me think of my dad once telling me about a dream he'd had of Heaven.

The more I thought about it, the more I wanted to go back, even though my more logical side said it probably *was* a vision of Heaven, for that's where I might end up if I was dumb enough to return.

This went on long enough that I was actually thinking of going back to see if there was such a place—a lake with flowers and all. Maybe it was my subconscious telling me I needed closure from such a traumatic event.

I finally decided I had to go back. I wouldn't have any peace if I didn't go and try to figure out what was going on. After all, I'd only seen a big shadow and some glowing eyes, and maybe a tree actually had fallen and someone had come along and helped me out later by righting the camper and removing the tree, maybe a forest worker.

So, I made plans to return to that old road on Marias Pass. I even decided I wanted to do a watercolor of that lake, assuming it was real. I started to get excited about it, some of my original optimism coming back, the idea I'd had of traveling and painting. I hadn't even gotten to see Glacier National Park.

But oh boy, was my daughter set against it. She's very protective of me, and she insisted I shouldn't go, and she was really upset when I told her I was taking the cats along. She made me promise to leave them. She even joked around and said I should make out a will, though I'm not sure she was kidding.

The night before I was going to leave, I felt restless and was having trouble sleeping. The cats were snuggled up next to me, as if they knew I would be leaving.

I finally drifted off, only to have a nightmare. Something was standing at my bedroom window, trying to see inside. It was big and dark and had glowing red eyes, and it seemed like it had come to tell me something, but I couldn't figure out what. When I woke, both cats were gone, and it took me awhile to find them—they were hiding under the bed. Had the dream been real? Or had my own fears and uncertainties affected them?

The next morning, my daughter Beth was at my door, trying to talk me out of going. She had her suitcase and was going to stay with the cats, as there was no way she would let me take them. She was carrying a map book, and she opened it and said, "Dad, take a look at this. I think this may have something to do with what you saw."

It was a *Montana Road and Recreation Atlas*, and she opened it to the page that showed the west side of Glacier National Park.

"This isn't all that far from where you were camped," Beth said. "At least not if you go cross-country."

She pointed to a section of map between the Trail of the Cedars and McDonald Falls that had a note that read: "Alleged Bigfoot Sighting, June 2003."

Now my son Darren showed up, carrying a small pack.

"We decided you're not going alone, Dad," he informed me. "I took a few days off work. I've been needing to get out, anyway."

I was really pleased to hear this, as I seldom got to spend any time with him, for he ran a busy welding shop.

"Looks like we're going Bigfooting," I grinned, though deep inside I was wondering if I really wanted him to get involved with all this.

We had a great talk on the way over, stopping in Missoula for lunch. While there, Darren pulled out the map book Beth had given me.

"Where exactly are we going?" He asked.

Taking the book, I studied it, then said, "I think it's this little road here." I showed him a small road near the top of the pass.

"Dad, this says Devil's Creek. Did you notice that?"

When Darren said that, I felt a chill come over me. Why would someone call something Devil's Creek? Had they had something strange happen there, just like I had? Was that the only word they could come up with to describe something they'd seen there? I knew these old names predated the name Bigfoot, and attributing it to the devil was a common way to describe such strangeness.

"I don't see any lakes very close to that road. Are you sure you want to go back?" Darren was now asking. "We could just go into Glacier and enjoy the park."

I felt confused. I wasn't sure what I wanted to do. I recalled the figure at my window the previous night. Had it been a dream? Was this all just some kind of strange hallucination?

"I don't know," I replied. "Let's decide when we get closer."

Well, it wasn't that much longer before we got to West Glacier. We stopped for some ice cream, but it was time to make that decision.

Going to Glacier would be a lot more fun, and we could drive across the Going to the Sun Road on over to St. Mary Lake and Goose Island, and I could probably get some good photos, which I could take home and use for inspiration for some watercolors. It seemed like the logical decision.

But then, from nowhere, came that peaceful feeling surrounding the lake. I knew I had to go back and see if it was real or was just my imagination. I knew Darren preferred to go into the park, but I felt I had no choice. Maybe we could go to the park afterwards.

We were soon at the old road, where we turned and went back

into the tall timber where I'd camped. We got out and looked around, but it didn't feel like anything different, just a camp spot in the trees.

"Let's go back in a ways see what we can find," I said.

It wasn't long before the road petered out at a small turnaround next to a creek. There was no lake, just some nice wild roses in bloom that would make a nice painting, so I took some pictures.

"Should we go now?" Darren asked.

As I poked around some, I found a small trail following the creek.

"Let's follow this trail for a ways," I replied. "It's possible this creek feeds from a lake, but I really don't want to go too far."

Darren now seemed reluctant. "Dad, I really didn't want to say anything, but this place kind of gives me the creeps."

I really wanted to respect Darren's feelings, but something was driving me on.

"Why don't you wait here in the truck?" I asked. "I won't be gone long."

Now Darren looked panicked.

"I'm not going to let you go alone," he replied. "But I don't think it's a good idea for either of us to go. Something's not right here, Dad. I don't think there's a lake up there. I wish I'd brought my drone."

I stood there as that peaceful feeling again came over me, and I wanted nothing more than to go on up to that lake. But I then recalled how I'd ignored my intuition when I'd first camped here, staying even though things seemed questionable. That hadn't turned out well, and I'd promised to never ignore my intuition again, yet here I was, doing the same thing again.

"You're right," I replied. "Let's go."

But now I started arguing with myself again. I was so close, why not go find that lake? Darren could wait here, it wouldn't take long, and if I could capture something so peaceful in a painting, it would sell really well, plus I would want to look at it myself, maybe hang it on my own wall. Shoot, I could maybe do a print of it and it would make lots of money. It would be so worth it...

Now Darren had my arm and was pulling me along, back to the

truck. I started pulling back, saying, "It won't take long, I'll be back soon. This is my last chance, you have to understand."

Now Darren whispered urgently, "Dad, there's something over there in the bushes. We have to go, *now*."

Even when hearing that, I didn't want to go. But my son is a lot bigger and stronger than me, and he pretty much strong-armed me back into the truck, quickly starting it and turning around.

To the bitter end, I wanted to go back. That mythical lake drew me to it, although later I realized there was no lake, and what was driving me wasn't what I thought.

Now Darren said quietly, and I could hear fear in his voice, "Dad, look back."

I turned and looked out the back window, where I saw a giant creature, covered head to toe in thick hair, looking malevolent and holding a large stick.

I knew then that my son had saved my life.

I also knew it was the closure I so badly needed, the knowledge that there was no peaceful lake, but that I had somehow been misled and was walking straight into a trap. And if Darren hadn't been there, I know I would've joined the ranks of those who have mysteriously disappeared in and around Glacier.

He drove us back to West Glacier, where we bought a park pass, then went to Apgar and had a snack, then drove up to Logan Pass, neither of us saying a word the entire time. Looking back, I think we were in some kind of shock.

The park was busy, and as we hiked the Hidden Lake Trail to the lake overlook, I normally would've been miserable surrounded by people, but it felt good for once.

Finally, standing at the end of the trail, high above the beautiful teal-blue lake, my eyes were drawn in the direction of Marias Pass, far beyond Reynolds Mountain, Gunsight Pass, and peaks with names like Dusty Star, Little Chief, and Citadel, far to a mythical lake that I still somehow wanted to exist.

But I knew I'd fallen victim to either my own imagination or some kind of strange mind control. I'll never know which, but I do know that Bigfoot is real, and I also know I'll never go camping anywhere near Marias Pass again.

Later, along with Darren and Beth, we worked out a plan. Beth would move into my house, taking care of the house and the cats while I rented a place for a few months wherever I wanted to go to paint. I would then come home and work on selling my paintings, then after a couple of months, I'd go back out somewhere new. This would save Beth having to pay rent, as well as giving me a home base and a stable place for the two cats. And if for some reason, my paintings didn't sell well enough to support that lifestyle, I would still have a home and could go back to handyman work. Darren and Beth could take care of any maintenance the house needed while I was gone.

So far, it's worked out well, and as soon as I leave my current place in Colorado, I'll go home to Spokane for a few months, then maybe go to Yosemite, which is a place I've always wanted to paint. And my paintings are selling well.

Sometimes I still imagine that peaceful lake and want to go there, but I've since discovered that happiness is pretty much in how one views things, not in a particular place.

I've since found many beautiful places where I can find peace, and I will add that I no longer argue with myself. If things feel questionable, I trust my instincts and just move along, for now I know that things aren't always what they seem.

4

EAT, DRINK, AND BE HAIRY

Our local outdoors club decided it was time to do a survival seminar, seeing how several of its members had become lost that summer, though all had managed to get themselves found with no harm done. The club brought in several experts in various fields to give talks, and both my wife Sarah and I decided that, given how we both work outdoors (she's a geologist), we should attend.

My favorite session was a talk by a woman named Helen, who was an expert in medicinal plants and had even written a book about them. She knew her stuff, and after her talk, Sarah had a question about something or other, which led to me asking Helen how she became interested in medicinal plants. When she asked if I wanted to hear what was behind it all, I said I did, so we went out and sat at a nearby picnic table, where she told us the following incredible story. I liked it partly because it contrasts so much with a lot of the stories I've heard about Bigfoot being angry and destructive.
—Rusty

. . .

Rusty, if you ever worry about being out in the wilds and needing help, let me tell you there's more out there than meets the eye. How do I know? Well, I learned through experience—a life and death experience.

But fortunately I had a rescuer—and a most unusual one, I'll add, one who probably knew more about medicinal plants than any other creature on Earth, other than his or her own kin, that is.

So, how did I end up out in the wilds needing help? Well, it was an experience that taught me a number of things and basically changed my entire outlook about life in general.

I was in my late 30s and had been working as a nurse practitioner in the oil field. You have to study medicine for a long time to become a nurse practitioner, and you have many of the same responsibilities as an actual physician, including being able to prescribe medicine. You do have legal limitations on what you can do, but a lot of nurse practitioners actually know almost as much as a doctor and can diagnose things very well. You don't make as much as a doctor, but you do make really good money, much more than a regular nurse in most cases.

But I hadn't studied nursing to get rich—I don't think anyone does—though I was making really good money at the time, especially working in the oil patch. Petroleum companies typically hire medical people to take care of their workers in some of the larger oil-patch facilities. It's kind of like being a school nurse in that you're on-site and ready for accidents or whatever, a presence to make sure workers have medical care in case of emergencies. Oil rigs and such can be dangerous places to work.

I was the only medical person on staff at a large oilsands operation in Alberta at the time, and I'd accumulated an ungodly number of vacation days. My boss basically told me I needed to take them or lose them, so I headed down across the border to Glacier National Park, a place I'd always wanted to visit. Being from Alberta, I'd seen plenty of beautiful mountains in our national parks of Banff and

Jasper, but I wanted to go visit the states and see the country down there.

I was also interested in the Museum of the Plains Indian over in Browning, near the east side of Glacier, there on the Blackfeet Reservation, as I've always had a curiosity about how the early indigenous people lived.

So, off I went. I first visited Waterton National Park just across the border from Glacier, then I crossed into the states on the Chief's Highway, which goes right by Chief Mountain, a sacred site for the Blackfeet. Most of the east side of Glacier borders the Blackfeet Reservation, with the town of Browning not far away, so I decided to first go to the museum there. It was well worth the drive, and I really enjoyed all the displays about the early indigenous people in the area.

One display really stood out—it was about the edible and medicinal plants the Blackfeet used. It was quite extensive, and I stood there for some time, studying what plants you could use to heal yourself. I had no idea that some of these very plants would soon be on my own survival menu.

Being a nurse, the topic of medicinal and edible plants was interesting to me, as I could see how people might use them when injured or lost. I decided to look into it more when I got back home and see what I could learn. I laugh in retrospect at how life can be so ironic— I was becoming interested in something that would soon help save my life, unbeknownst to me.

I next decided to visit that part of Glacier National Park known as Many Glacier, since I was already on that side of the park. I had my camping gear with me and managed to get a site at the campground, which was first come first-served. It was mid-August, still a popular time in the park, so I felt very lucky.

I paid for three nights, talked with the campground host for awhile, then set up my tent and proceeded to make myself a nice dinner of lasagna I'd bought earlier at the small grocery store in Browning, along with a nice salad and cup of tea. I recalled that meal many times in my mind's eye later, desperately wishing for just one bite.

Even though the campground was nearly full, everyone was quiet, and I spent one of the nicest nights of my life there, first sitting in my camp chair watching the stars unfold above the high mountaintops, then finally crawling into my roomy tent and falling asleep on my comfy sleeping pad in my new sleeping bag. It all felt luxurious, which may sound strange since I was camping, but you have to remember I'd been living in a trailer in an oil-patch man-camp with nothing but noise and people coming and going. I felt like I'd found paradise.

The next morning, I relaxed again in my camp chair, eating a breakfast of scrambled eggs and toast, all cooked over my little Coleman stove. I again kind of luxuriated in my good fortune at being there. Little did I know it would be the last meal I'd have for some time.

Many Glacier is central to a lot of nice hikes, and I studied the map, deciding to hike to nearby Fishercap Lake. After putting together a day pack, I next made a grave mistake by going to the campground host and paying for another four nights, making my stay a total of a week.

Why was this a mistake? Well, it pretty much guaranteed that no one would miss me for some time, as I was all paid up. If I'd left it at three nights, the host would've noticed I'd overstayed my reservation and contacted the rangers, who would then send out a search party. As it was, I'm sure they thought I was just out hiking, leaving early and getting back late, thinking nothing of my absence.

So, off I set to hike to nearby Fishercap Lake, just a short distance on a fairly easy trail. I'd been told there were a lot of moose there, and I thought it would be fun to get some photos. I hadn't been hiking a lot, so I wasn't in the greatest of shape, and I figured I'd start out slow. This trail would be perfect, as I could just cruise along, then come back to the campground and be lazy.

I was soon at the lake, hiding behind a stand of willows, watching a young moose stick its head under the waters and come up with a mouthful of vegetation. A couple came and stood nearby, and we got to talking quietly, so as to not disturb the moose. They told me I should hike on up to Redrock Falls, which wasn't much farther and was worth the trek. It was only 1.8 miles from the falls to the parking lot, and I was already partway there.

I wasn't a bit tired, so I decided to go on up there. A number of people were on the trail, which made me feel safe, as I knew solo hiking in Glacier wasn't advised because of bears. In retrospect, it was kind of ironic at how cautious I was being, like someone from a city, not someone from the deep woods of Canada, where there are lots of bears.

The trail was still easy, and I was really enjoying the hike. It didn't take long to get to the falls, and I decided it would be a great place to spend the afternoon, much better than down at the campground. The views of Mt. Grinnell and the other massive peaks were enough to entertain me for hours.

I made myself comfortable, leaning against a rock, watching a ground squirrel collecting grass for its winter supply, then I promptly fell asleep! I guess the trip and activity was wearing on me, or maybe I'd finally realized I was on vacation and could really relax.

When I woke, the last traces of sunset lit up the high peaks above me, and the shadows were long, telling me I should be on my way. I was now alone, everyone else having the sense to get back before it got dark. I grabbed my daypack and water bottle and headed back the way I'd come, knowing I needed to hurry or I'd soon be hiking in the dark.

Now, everyone should always carry a headlamp or flashlight when they're out hiking, even if it's just a short trek, and I know that now, but let's just say it was something I learned the hard way. I didn't do any hiking up by Ft. McMurray, where the oil-sands camp was, for it was thick timber and muskeg with nowhere to go.

I was now nearly running, trying to beat the light, when I must've snagged my toe on a root or something, because before I knew it, I went down. I fell forward, and I instinctively tried to catch myself with my hands. I knew instantly that I'd made a mistake, for I felt both wrists snap at the same time.

I immediately knew both wrists were broken. Ironically, I'd treated a guy a year before for the same injury. He'd caught his foot on the edge of a trailer and gone down and done the exact same thing, shattering his wrists. It had been a painful time for him, and he'd ended up on leave for four months, unable to do much of anything until he healed.

I sat there in a state of disbelief, then began examining my situation in a kind of detached way. My hands were at a 45-degree angle to my arms and were swelling rapidly. I could still wiggle my fingers and there were no bone protrusions, so I hoped it wasn't as bad as it felt.

As I lay there on the trail, I knew I had only a small timeframe before the pain would become severe and possibly even incapacitating. I needed to get myself up and get help before I went into shock. I had to get back to the parking lot, which was near some cabins and a motel.

Have you ever tried to stand without using your hands? It's extremely difficult, especially when you're in the middle of a trail with nothing to wedge yourself against. I tried and tried, using my elbows to try to lift myself up, but each time, I felt like I was going to pass out.

I finally realized I was going to have to scoot over to the edge of the trail where I could brace myself against a tree. I managed to scoot along on my rear, but I misjudged the edge and rolled right off the trail, down into a stand of huckleberry bushes.

I managed to hit one of my wrists on something in the process, and the pain was so intense I must've passed out, for I don't recall anything until I woke in the middle of the night, moaning.

It took some time to recall where I was and what had happened, and I don't remember a lot about that night, except that my hands and wrists had become so swollen I couldn't move them at all. I could no longer even wiggle my fingers, and the pain was intense. I now wondered if I wasn't going to die from hypothermia, as I was shivering.

I miraculously made it through the night, though I remember falling into a fitful sleep off and on, waking occasionally and wondering why I didn't just die and get it over with. It seemed ironic how quickly my happiness at being there had turned into tragedy and what seemed like my own imminent death.

OK, my first mistake was not having a light and my second mistake was misjudging the edge of the trial, but I was now about to make my third mistake, which was even worse than the first two.

As it became daylight and I was finally alert enough to realize what was going on, I tried to crawl back up to the trail, using my elbows, but it was too painful, as well as too steep.

When I realized there was no way I was going to get back on the trail, I should've stayed where I was and yelled when I heard people go by, and I'm sure I would've been rescued within hours. But instead, I decided I needed to get down by the stream and put my hands and wrists in the cold water to reduce the swelling. I recalled that when the oil-sands worker had broken his wrists, the first thing I'd done was wrap them in bags of ice, which helped with both the pain and the swelling.

So, scooting myself down to the stream was my third big mistake, for once down there, no one could hear me yelling because of the sound of the nearby falls. I'd initially been close to the trail where someone might've heard me, but now my chances were zero.

I realized this after I was down there and my thoughts had cleared, the pain being relieved somewhat by the cold water. In fact, the water was so cold I had to be careful to not actually freeze my wrists and hands, taking them out every so often.

And I also realized that I'd gotten myself to where I not only would never be heard by anyone but also where I'd never be seen because of the stand of huckleberries. I'd gone from the proverbial frying pan into the fire, and the only good thing about it was that I could now get the swelling down, as well as lean over and drink from the stream, lapping up the water like a dog.

I then realized I'd made mistake number four—I'd left my pack above on the trail where I'd fallen, the same pack that had trail mix and fruit and a couple of sandwiches. But I finally decided it didn't matter, as I wouldn't have been able to open the pack to get to the food anyway.

As the day wore on, I yelled and yelled, hoping someone would hear me, but the roar from the falls was just too loud. Redrock Falls is actually a series of small falls, so the noise is constant and continues for some ways.

All that day, I drifted in and out of consciousness from the pain, and when I was feeling lucid enough to recognize what was going on, I would drift into an inconsolable sadness, wondering if anyone would ever find my body—so close to the trail, yet so far.

I would sometimes think about my family, my friends, my past, and all my future dreams—my hopes of going on a Doctors without Borders mission to help sick people, things like that.

After what seemed like several cycles of day and night, I was beginning to feel weaker and weaker. I knew I needed food, but I also had no appetite, which was probably a good thing, as there was nothing to eat anyway. I knew if I was in better shape, maybe I wouldn't need my arms to stand, but I'd tried everything, from wedging myself against a tree to even sliding around on my rear end to a small rise, where I used gravity to help me get on my legs, but promptly fell back down, almost again hitting my wrists.

Finally, I recall waking one morning to something pushing its wet nose on my face, then opening my eyes to see a fox, of all things. It looked at me with what I interpreted as sad eyes, maybe wondering why I was there. By then, I'd given up all hope and was wishing death would come and get it over with.

But seeing the fox's shining eyes and silky coat filled me with wonder, and I knew it was aware I was in trouble. For some reason, that little fox left me with a renewed will to live.

Well, I could add more, but I think you get the picture. I later figured out I'd been there about four days when I had what I call the dream, though I don't know if it was a dream or if it really happened. If it was real, I barely even saw who or what visited me.

I'd yelled so much I was hoarse and had a sore throat, and like I mentioned, I was getting very weak, though fortunately I had plenty of water. Humans can live for three or four weeks without food, so I'm told, but only a few days without water, so I was lucky to be near the stream, if you want to call sabotaging myself by rolling off the trail any kind of luck.

Finally, despairing of trying to deal with the constant pain and unable to get myself up off the ground, I finally just kind of lost it. I went into a tirade about how I didn't want to die like this and how it wasn't fair for someone who'd dedicated their life to helping others to die without help and on and on. This was followed by a round of yelling and sobbing and just letting it all go.

I then settled back and suddenly felt at peace with everything. I guess I'd gone through denial and then on to acceptance at that point. I drifted off, and when I woke it was dusk, though I'm still not sure I was actually awake and it wasn't just a dream—or maybe I was hallucinating. But there, in the evening shadows, I saw a huge form coming towards me, pushing its way through the trees and bushes.

As it got closer, I could feel my hackles go up, for it looked like a huge grizzly bear, larger than anything I'd ever seen, even in the Canadian bush. It was hard to tell because of the lack of light, but I could finally see it wasn't a bear after all, but was walking on two legs and had a human-like face.

Now this large creature came to my side and bent over, holding out what looked like a small flat pancake. I was of course unable to take it, and I just looked at it questioningly, afraid to move. It was close enough that I could see its face was covered with dark skin and its eyes were really big and liquid looking.

He, or maybe it was a she, I don't know, then put this small cake up to my lips, as if wanting me to eat it. I took a bite, and it was really crusty, but as I slowly chewed it, it actually tasted pretty good, though it had a somewhat bitter aftertaste. I slowly ate the entire thing, and I imagined the creature looked pleased, though I could barely see it. It then turned and left.

I immediately went into a deep sleep, and when I woke, it was daylight. Miraculously, the pain had lessened, and it looked like the swelling had gone down.

I then noticed a small pile of what looked like raspberries nearby. Not being able to use my hands, I finally managed to scoot over next to them and basically lick them up, again like a dog might do. I've never had anything taste so delicious, and I found out later they're called loganberries. I then scooted back to the stream and put my wrists back in the cold water for awhile, then slept.

That evening, again at deep dusk, the creature returned with another of the cakes. It again held the cake for me as I ate it, and it was then that I realized the bitter taste had to be salicylic acid, the main ingredient of aspirin and what relieves pain, fever, and inflammation. I've since learned that willows and other plants naturally contain salicylic acid and were used extensively by the natives for treating pain and swelling.

The creature also had some huckleberries, which it slowly fed me. As it did so, I tried to study it more closely, but it was so dark it was hard to see much.

It then walked around behind me, and for a brief moment I was scared at what it might do, but it gently picked me up and carried me back up to the trail. I was certain it would leave me there, but it didn't. It actually carried me all the way back to the parking lot.

By then, it was pitch dark, and there was no one around. It took me to the step of one of the nearby cabins, where it gently put me down.

What it did next, I'll never forget. Stepping back into the trees, it let out the most horrific howl I've ever heard. It was so loud I wanted to put my hands over my ears, which of course I couldn't.

I could now hear people inside talking, and I started yelling at the best of my ability, which wasn't very loud, as I was so weak. But I guess it was loud enough, for they tentatively opened the door, and upon seeing me, helped me inside. I knew then that the creature had slipped into the trees and was gone.

Everything after that is kind of a blur, though I do remember going to an emergency room, where the ER staff quickly carried me to a bed, hooked me up with saline and morphine, wheeled me into an x-ray room where they took multiple x-rays, then knocked me out to straighten and splint both wrists. When I woke, I had no idea who I was, where I was, or what had been done, which I think was a good thing.

I spent two weeks in a rehab facility, then went to stay in an apartment in Calgary my company rented for me, where I had constant care for several months until I could use my hands again. It was a long slow frustrating process, but fortunately there was no permanent damage.

I eventually returned to work, where I started studying medicinal plants in my free time. There's a lot more to the topic than one could learn in a lifetime, and I eventually quit my job to go study with some of the indigenous people in western Canada, writing a book about it in an effort to help preserve their knowledge. I now live in White-horse in the Yukon, where I again work as a nurse, but also work with the natives to try and preserve their heritage and culture.

There's not a whole lot more to my story, except that I sometimes wonder why the creature didn't take me to the cabins when it first found me, but instead waited a day. Maybe it thought I could go on my own after eating one of the cakes. Or maybe there was something else going on, like a bear on the trail. I'll never know.

I just feel very fortunate it helped me, but I still sometimes wonder if I didn't somehow rescue myself and dreamed everything else up. It's just hard to imagine something like that actually exists, I guess.

And now, when I sit and look out into the Yukon wilderness, I'm not afraid, but my whole perspective has changed. I guess you could say my sense of the mundane has been replaced by a sense of wonder, for I now know there's more out there than we could ever understand. And I guess that can be a good thing, depending on one's perspective. I know it turned out to be a good thing for me—a very good thing.

5
TERROR IN THE TOWER

I'll never forget the evening I got a call sitting on the porch of my little cabin in Colorado while taking a few days off from fishing. Actually, it was more like I didn't have any fishing clients, as the season was getting off to a slow start.

This guy named Brian had heard I collected Bigfoot stories and had looked up my number, wanting to share his experience with me, partly to see if I knew of anything like it, which I didn't.

We talked for a long time that evening, long after I would normally sit outside, as the mosquitoes can get bad. I found his story kind of unsettling, but not all that far removed from some of the more hair-raising things I've heard coming out of Glacier. I don't know if Bigfoot are as intelligent as humans or not, but his theory is interesting—and a bit scary, if true.
—Rusty

Rusty, I have a theory that I've never heard anyone else ever mention, though I doubt if I'm the first to come up with it. It requires that you believe in Bigfoot, which I know a lot of people don't.

Now, I personally do, but only because of the incident I'm about to tell you about. But before that, I was as skeptical as they come. After all, as a fire lookout in one of the most rugged and remote national parks in the United States, if anyone should see them, it would be me—and I hadn't, even after 20 summers in lookout towers.

I'd seen every other kind of critter out there, including the elusive wolverine, which very few have ever seen. Oh, and I've seen several lynx, which the biologists didn't even think still lived in Glacier. But Bigfoot? Ha! A giant ape running around the forests? Fat chance. How could something that big hide, and what would they eat?

After all, the area already has over 700 grizzlies, plus probably easily that number of black bears. How do I know that? Well, the park and some other groups did a bunch of studies using thousands of hair samples from bears, samples collected from strands of barbed wire attached to trees. They found that 765 grizzly bears live in the region, and most are concentrated in and around Glacier.

So, if you add the black bears to the grizzlies, you have at least 1,000 bears trying to find eats in the area, and that's a lot of food, considering how much a bear can consume. I figured that Bigfoot, if they really were as large as everyone says, would need more food than a grizzly, and how much could one ecosystem maintain? Even if Bigfoot were herbivores, it would still take a lot of food. And did they hibernate? What would they eat in the winter if they didn't?

The whole topic seemed ludicrous to me, and after spending so many hours in a lookout tower scanning the forest with a scope, if Bigfoot existed, I'd be the most likely person on the planet to spot one—and I hadn't. Hours and hours and hours in a tower with a scope, and not one Bigfoot. In fact, I'd never even heard anything that could possibly be one—not one howl or woodknock or that famous siren call they supposedly make. And I was friends with all the other lookouts, and none of them had ever seen one, either.

So, back to my theory, but first, let me ask you this. If you were someone who was trying to hide in the forest, could you do it? I bet very few people could, but I know there are some who can. You'd need to be stealthy, especially if your life depended on it. It's probably something you'd get good at if you had to.

I remember reading about some guy in the woods back East somewhere who lived for some 20 years in the forest near a town and stole camper's food and even their supplies, but nobody knew he was there. That's a long time to go undetected. And there are other stories like that of people living not that far out and yet nobody knows they're there.

So, my point is that yes, people can effectively hide in the woods. We're not as big as Bigfoot, but we're not exactly small, either. And someone could even evade a lookout scope if they knew where to go and where not to go.

So, I at first thought I'd see Bigfoot if they existed from my vantage point high on the ridge, but I then started thinking that maybe they were good at hiding. If they knew where humans hung out, they could avoid such places and never be seen.

One thing that sets humans apart from other animals is our ability to adapt to different situations. That's why we're the ultimate invasive species—we can go anywhere and survive, and we've basically invaded the entire planet. If you think about it, it's kind of amazing, as we're really gimpy physically—no big teeth or claws—but we're smart and know how to make tools. I was beginning to think maybe Bigfoot was smart, but could they make tools? Not a chance.

So, I spent a lot of hours in my lookout thinking about all this, as you might guess. I had a good friend who claimed he'd seen a Bigfoot over by Swan Lake, not too far from Glacier, and his story seemed authentic, though I was a skeptic. He wasn't a lookout, but he was an honest guy, not one to make up stuff, so it really got me to thinking.

And so, these things ran through my mind. When you're in a lookout tower, there's lots of time to think.

So, my theory goes like this. Everyone says Bigfoot is an ape, maybe even something descended from Gigantopithecus, that giant ape they found a jawbone and some teeth from. Everything I've read, everyone I've talked to, just assumes Bigfoot's an ape, related to humans, but in a distant way. If you look at the biology, humans and apes are related, but it goes way back.

But what if Bigfoot is actually closer to our family tree, maybe something like Neanderthal, something not so distant? What if they have brains that compare to ours and can think like us? We're finding more and more evidence that Neanderthal were really smart. Maybe Bigfoot is like some of the hominid species we studied in school, like Homo Erectus—not so far removed from us? If they can think like a human, like we do, they could thereby figure out how to elude us.

OK, back to my fire tower experience, the reason I now believe Bigfoot exists and is very close to being human. But first, some history about where I was.

Glacier's a big park, and it's seen its share of fires. It was established in 1910, and in the park's first decade, an average of 30,000 acres of forest burned each year. Because of this, it became the first national park to establish fire-fighting procedures, and part of this included fire-lookout towers.

The park built 17 such towers in the 1930s, mostly all two-story wooden structures with a windowless dirt floor storage area, topped by a small room in which the fire lookouts worked and lived.

Of that 17, only four are still manned—Huckleberry Mountain, Numa Ridge, Scalplock Mountain, and Swiftcurrent Mountain. My job was manning the Numa Ridge lookout over on the northwest side of the park near Bowman Lake.

The side of the park I was on is the drainage for the North Fork of the Flathead River and is probably the least visited part of the park because it's hard to get into. You need a good high-clearance vehicle, and the road is bumpy and narrow and long.

And of course, we're only maybe 20 or 30 miles from the Canadian border, which is even less inhabited and has lots of rugged country. Biologists say this region is possibly the most significant in the entire country for predator habitat, which means it's fairly untouched. And when you're manning a lookout tower up there, it feels like you're the only human on the planet.

Now, as you can probably imagine, lookout duty can get really boring. You spend the day scanning the countryside looking for smoke, sometimes just casually looking, and sometimes through a scope, but other than that, you have no real duties. The most exciting thing that ever happens is when a big storm comes through and you're in the thick of it, lightning popping all around while you wonder if the tower's going to get hit, which is quite an experience when it does, even with a lightning rod on the roof.

Then the storm moves on through, and you're left trying to spot any fires that may have been started by lightning. Sometimes they smolder for days, so you have to stay on it long after the storm's gone, constantly watching and being alert.

But most of your time is spent keeping an eye out, nothing happening, bored, with only so many books you can read, only so many games of Solitaire before you feel like you're going stir crazy, even though you're out in the most beautiful place on Earth and wouldn't want to be anywhere else.

Ten days of this, then you get a break and can go out and get resupplied, take a shower, eat a real meal at some cafe, do your laundry, talk to some real human beings (as opposed to those in your head), then go right back out.

Of course, it being Glacier, occasionally some intrepid hiker will show up at the tower wanting to ask a gazillion questions and take photos, usually of themselves with you on the tower stairs, which you gladly agree to do for the chance to talk to someone.

And this is pretty much what started everything, a yahoo named Mark who came to see if he could raise hell, which he did. I'm kind of joking about the raising hell thing, because I don't think he had any idea what came from his visit, though I'm pretty sure that's what started it all.

So, it's a nice sunny day, no storms to be seen, and here comes this young guy maybe in his late-twenties and very fit, which you have to be to hike the 5.6 mile long trail, which gains almost 3,000 feet in elevation. It's a stiff hike, and even though I did it every couple of weeks, it would still get to me, though going out was relatively easy, being all downhill.

So, I'm in the tower studying a distant meadow that looks kind of smoky, trying to figure out if it's just mist or actual smoke, when I hear this guy shouting from below. The tower has a small deck which connects to the stairs, so I go out to see what's going on.

Well, this guy's down there yelling, wanting to come up into the tower, saying something about trying to spot his buddy. Now, all the towers have a metal chain you can put across the staircase leading up to the lookout area, along with a "Private" sign. We put these up when we need privacy, for various reasons. I had my sign up, as I wasn't in the mood for visitors, but this guy just took it down and came on up.

I was pretty torqued, but at least he tapped on the window before barging in. He was such a happy-go-lucky guy and so enthusiastic, I didn't even get a chance to say anything before he's offering me a beer.

Not many hikers carry beer, and it was a rare treat for me, so I obliged and let him come in. He asked all kinds of questions, fascinated, then said his name was Mark, and he wanted to sign up to be a lookout.

I seriously had never seen anyone so enthused about being a lookout, though lots of people ask about it. And I'll jump ahead and say he was serious, as I ran into him the following season down in Apgar, and he told me he was manning the Huckleberry tower. I didn't have the heart to tell him what happened after he left.

The views at Numa Ridge are stupendous, and Mark wanted to know the names of everything, so I pointed out Rainbow Peak, Square Peak, Mount Carter, Bowman Lake, Akokala Lake, and Long Bow Lake, along with some other peaks and such. I really took a liking to this guy, and since he wanted to see if he could spot his friend fishing down by Bowman Lake, I showed him how to use the scope.

Bowman Lake's too far away to actually see anyone fishing, so that was a disappointment, I guess, until he said he could see two guys over in a small meadow on a distant hillside.

I took a look, and sure enough, there were two guys in this remote patch of green, a small clearing in the forest. They were far enough away that I couldn't make out much, but they seemed to be digging for something. It seemed really odd to me, for in order to get to where they were, they'd have to do some serious bushwhacking.

Mark was back on the scope, and he got all agitated and said there was a bear heading their way. I took another look, and sure enough, I could make out a bear heading for the clearing. There wasn't anything we could do about it, so I just watched, hoping they had bear spray.

Mark went out on the deck and started yelling in their direction, which I thought was a pretty hopeless thing to do, given how far away they were.

But now I could see them stop and look our way. I was incredulous. The wind must be carrying his voice just right, or else they had extremely acute hearing. They quickly disappeared into the trees.

All this took only a few minutes, but it left me with an odd feeling. What were they doing over there? Backcountry campers need permits in Glacier, and even at that, you're only allowed to camp in certain areas. I knew there was no trail or camping where they were, and they didn't even appear to have packs or any gear. And digging was totally illegal, as was any kind of disturbance in the park.

Well, Mark hung around for awhile, then headed back down the trail to Bowman Lake. As he left, I had the strangest feeling, kind of a premonition almost, that I should go down with him. I generally liked my job as a lookout, the privacy and solitude and beauty, but I suddenly had the feeling that things weren't as they should be. Call it a hunch, but I'm pretty sure in retrospect that it was from the two figures we saw.

As I watched Mark head back, I started wondering again what the pair was doing way over in that little clearing. Why had they slipped into the forest upon hearing Mark yell? Or had they even heard him? Maybe the timing was just a coincidence, and they'd instead realized a bear was nearby.

The rest of the day was quiet, no visitors, and when evening came, I found myself not wanting to take my usual short hike to stretch my legs, but instead wanted to just stay in the tower. It felt secure. I figured I felt that way from seeing the bear, but then, I see bears every so often from up there and have never felt that way.

Now, the Numa Ridge lookout has a heavy wooden panel with 200 spikes driven into it that you can drop into place on the stairway for protection from grizzlies. I didn't usually do this, as it's heavy and a real pain to do, but that night, I dropped it into place.

Sometimes I would listen to my little battery-operated radio in the evenings while watching the sunset, but that night, I pretty much hunkered down and kept a low profile. I even got out my shotgun. At the time, guns weren't legal in the park (they are now, but only if unloaded), and I don't know if any other lookouts had arms, but I suspected they did. You kind of feel like a sitting duck up in a tower. I also had bear spray, but I'll just say the gun wasn't for bears, and let it go at that.

Sometimes at night I would go out on the deck and watch the stars, look for satellites and the space station, that kind of thing, and even the Aurora Borealis, if I wanted to stay up late enough for it to get really dark. Being that far north, the days were long in the summer.

But that night, all I wanted to do was hide out in the corner of the lookout. Everything felt different, even creepy, which wasn't a feeling I normally had.

I'd recently started keeping a journal on the advice of a friend, who said I would someday enjoy reading about it all. Even though I told her there was nothing to write about, I'd started jotting down a few feelings and observations here and there, and reading it later, that night's entry read:

"No idea why, but I suddenly feel like things have changed, and not for the better. My peace of mind seems gone, replaced by some kind of deep fear, and I don't even know what it is I'm afraid of. All I can think of is getting out. If things aren't better by morning, I'm heading down. Maybe I just need a break."

Well, I dozed off thinking of being back home on my parents' farm in eastern Montana, out on the prairie, the house surrounded by tall trees, grasslands as far as the eye can see. I recalled all the times I'd watched big storms far away, fascinated by the huge anvil-shaped clouds rising over the distant horizon with their huge bolts of lightning, so far away you couldn't hear the thunder—except this time, I could.

I woke with a start, realizing I'd been dreaming, but I soon knew it wasn't a dream—I could hear bolts of lightning hitting the ground nearby. Oh boy, there's nothing like being in a tower during a lightning storm, but I'd been totally unaware anything was coming in. I have a weather radio and there hadn't been anything forecast.

As I lay there on my cot in my sleeping bag, I realized there wasn't any light with the strikes. I wasn't hearing thunder, but rather, it sounded like something was whacking on the tower itself. I immediately thought of the bear we'd seen earlier, but I'd never heard of a bear whacking on a building like that, though there was nothing that would keep them from doing so. I'd seen them whack on old logs to dislodge grubs lots of times.

Let me describe the tower here for a minute so you know what it was like. First, it's square, with five windows on each side, and the deck goes all the way around. It's basically two stories high, so you're not climbing a lot of stairs to get into it, like a lot of lookout towers.

The bottom story is made of wood, and there's not really any place one could climb up into the tower except by the stairs, and like I said, I'd dropped the spike board. And even if you could climb the walls, the deck, which jutted out, would stop you. I haven't been back up there since all this happened, but I've been told it now has solar panels along one side, but when I was there, it was all old-school and we didn't have any of the new high-tech equipment the lookouts now have.

So, I was lying there, listening to this whacking sound, when I realized the tower was actually shaking a bit. That made me stop and think, I can tell you, for the towers in Glacier aren't up on stilts like some, but have solid foundations. Whatever was hitting the tower was putting some strength into it.

My next thought was to wonder why a bear would do this. And let me add that the whole thing had a really malevolent feel to it, not like some bear just messing round, but rather like something trying to psych me out.

Does that sound paranoid enough for you? I actually lay there wondering if I wasn't going nuts. I'd heard stories about lookouts going crazy from the solitude and having to quit. In fact, there was a story that made the rounds about some guy over in the Swiftcurrent tower that had radioed dispatch saying he was watching little green guys get out of a UFO right below the tower. He later said he was kidding, but you don't call dispatch for a practical joke, as it will get you fired. He didn't get fired because he quit shortly thereafter.

I thought of those little green guys that night, then had to laugh at myself. Someone with the technology to come to Earth wouldn't be whacking the tower with a stick or whatever, they'd be able to come and go as they willed with jetpacks or whatnot.

My next thought was that someone had come up during the night and was trying to scare me. I was about ready to call dispatch, but something told me to keep quiet and just see what happened. But I can assure you I had my shotgun ready.

Now, let's segue back to my theory about Bigfoot being human-like here for a minute. What happened next was pretty human-like, in my book. The whacking stopped, and I could now hear talking. It was the strangest thing I've ever heard, and I wish there had been some way to record it.

Imagine someone who spoke a language that was as foreign-sounding to English as possible, something with different sounds to it, even popping noises, then throw in an English word every so often. It's like someone is speaking your language, yet they're not.

You strain to understand, as it sounds kind of familiar, but the words aren't in any kind of sequence to make sense, and they're also formed with strange vowels and such. I can't really describe it, but it was just plain weird. It almost sounded like a record being played backwards, if you've ever heard that.

So, I was still there on my cot, though I'd kicked off my sleeping bag and was up on my elbows, listening for all I was worth, trying to understand what was going on. I strained to hear it all, to make sense, but after awhile, it dawned on me that it was something totally out of my range of experience.

I finally figured out what was happening, that someone was trying to make me think they were speaking English. And next, they started knocking on the side of the tower, like it was a door, and I heard a guttural voice say, "Open up! Police!"

Well, that got me, but just for a second. I was actually starting to stand up, which would mean they could then see me through the windows, as there was enough moonlight, but I quickly lay back down.

Police? Up here? Not likely. And if there were law-enforcement around, it would be park rangers. What the heck was going on?

I then decided someone had come up during the night, or maybe they'd been hiding, but they were playing a little trick on me, or maybe even worse, they wanted me dead. That's actually what it felt like.

I reached down and grabbed my shotgun, which was under my cot, and, realizing it wasn't loaded, picked up a shell and loaded it into the chamber, snapping the slide shut, racking it. Now, that's a very distinctive sound, and most people would instantly know what it was, or even if they had never heard a shotgun being racked, they'd know something was up.

Nope, no effect at all. They either didn't know what a shotgun was or had no fear of it. I wasn't sure what to do next. I didn't want to shoot someone, and even if it was justified as self-defense, I knew I'd end up in trouble for having a gun in the park. It then dawned on me that all the windows were closed, so maybe they hadn't heard it, but I could hear them just fine, so that couldn't be it.

I knew I could go out on the deck and yell at them or something, but it seemed foolish, and I still felt that deep sense of dread. I'm no coward, but my instincts were telling me to stay inside and hunker down.

Back to the human-like thing. What they did next was to start crying. It was the most pitiful sound, just like a little baby, and I wondered if maybe they didn't actually have a baby out there. I mean, how could someone with a low guttural voice now sound like a tiny little baby? I'll admit, they almost got me with that one, as I started wondering if they hadn't somehow kidnapped someone's baby and was going to harm it.

But I ignored it, my sense of dread growing. Whoever this was, they were cunning and devious, and they seemed to know that a human baby in danger would get results, though I didn't fall for it.

I finally decided I needed to call dispatch and somehow get help. At that point, I didn't care if they thought I was nuts, as I knew I would be leaving and not coming back anyway, assuming I survived the night.

I tried to stay low as I went to the radio and keyed it on. The static was loud, and I turned the volume down, as I didn't want whoever was below to hear what I was saying. In a nutshell, I told Craig, the night dispatcher, that someone was trying to break into the tower and I needed backup. No, I hadn't been drinking, they knew I didn't drink (an occasional beer didn't count), and yes, I felt like I was in serious danger.

Well, this conversation was all in my head, because as I started to key dispatch, I realized it would be hopeless, as they wouldn't send anyone out at night anyway because of bear danger, not unless I'd broken my leg or something. After all, I was pretty secure up in the tower, and Craig knew I was armed. The whole conversation would go south, and I'd have to explain everything in the morning, and it wouldn't do any good anyway.

I was on my own.

Well, that's when I turned and saw the face in the window. I was shocked—both by the fact that they'd managed to climb the wall, but also by what I saw. And as I turned, I saw a second face in the window behind me.

Just as an aside, I found out later that they hadn't actually climbed the wall, but had leaned a dead tree against the deck, then somehow scaled it. They had to be strong to move a log that big, and they had to be very agile to climb it, is all I can say.

But back to the face. Let me describe what I saw—it's not something one's mind can easily grasp. Sure, if it was in some horror movie, you'd think what a great job the makeup guys had done, and you would know it wasn't real. But in real life? Not so easy. Your mind refuses to process it.

First, let me say they weren't huge, like a lot of Bigfoot stories you hear. They were larger than an average guy, sure, but not anything you'd stop and stare at if you saw one on the street—size wise, anyway, though you would definitely stop. They were actually kind of wiry. But the reason you'd stop is because of the face.

Now, the tower windows are tall and I could see their hairy bodies as well as their faces. They weren't all that hairy like in some Bigfoot accounts, where people say the hair flows. Their hair was more like what you'd see on a deer or something, short and stiff.

They had some facial hair, but not like a beard, but more like all over, except where their eyes were, and pretty short hair, at that. But those eyes, man, those eyes. They were terrifying, because they were large and black and yet they had some kind of glow to them, sort of like a backlight or something. Not red or green like you read about.

It was dark enough, even with the moonlight, that I couldn't really make out any facial expressions, but I somehow knew they meant me harm. I didn't need to see any teeth or ugly scowls to know that, I could just feel it deep inside. And later, as I thought about all this more, I wondered if they hadn't somehow telepathed it to me or even produced some kind of ultrasound, like I've read about in some Bigfoot accounts. I don't know, but I did feel very threatened.

My next thought was of how easily they could break out a window and come inside. I edged my way to the corner of the room, then held up my shotgun, thinking maybe if they saw it and realized what it was, they would leave. I was beginning to wonder if I weren't just having some kind of nightmare.

I was shocked to see them both take off quicker than you can say sic 'em. They obviously knew what a gun was.

I stood there, shaking, thinking it was going to be a long night, even if they didn't come back. There was no way I could sleep.

I wondered if maybe I should start getting my stuff packed up and ready to go. The only problem was, it was dark inside and there was no way I was going to turn on my headlamp. It would just make me a sitting duck, assuming they hadn't actually left, which something told me was indeed the case.

I finally slumped down in the corner, tired and half-asleep, and next thing I knew, I could see the dawn lighting up the distant peaks. I couldn't believe I'd survived. Had it all been a dream?

I slipped out of my longjohns into my clothes and started packing my gear, which didn't take long. I finally settled down enough to have some breakfast, and as I sat there, drinking coffee and eating some bagels and fruit, I tried to quiet my mind enough to make sure leaving was really what I should do.

If I walked out on my job mid-season, it would leave the park with no lookout along this northern region, which would be a bad thing. But maybe they could get someone else to come up, maybe even Mark, who'd been so excited about being a lookout. After all, it wasn't a skilled job, you just had to be self-sufficient and alert.

Or maybe I should just take a break for a few days and then come back up myself. I could tell everyone I'd been sick or something. What would I do if I wasn't a lookout? It had been my seasonal job for many years, and I couldn't afford to not work.

I decided to head out, then make up my mind once I got back down and into civilization, as the thought of coming back up and potentially having another night like I'd just had wasn't very appealing.

I think I was still kind of hoping it had just been a bad dream at that point—in fact, it still didn't seem real. Maybe I could clear my head by getting out of there for awhile, then come back, though the thought of doing so gave me the creeps.

I finally had my gear together. I radioed dispatch to tell them I was coming out, that I was sick. They were concerned, but I told them I was pretty sure I could do the hike down, as it was pretty easy, not like coming up.

I locked the tower, then removed the spike board and went on down the stairs, wary, looking all around, shotgun in hand, but I saw nothing out of the usual, except the big log still leaning against the deck. I pushed it down, and it made a big thud.

It was then that I realized how heavy it was. Two humans couldn't have lifted it and set it against the deck like that, unless they were weight lifters, and even then, it would be difficult. It gave me pause, and the fact that it hadn't been a dream finally set in.

I turned to go when I saw something had been etched into the side of the tower, the lighter wood standing out against the dark-brown paint. I was already getting a queasy feeling, wanting badly to flee, but I had to go see what it was.

As I walked over to the tower, what I saw was beyond strange. There, carved into the wood, was what I took to be a symbol, for what else could it be?

Now, back yet again to my theory about these creatures being hominids close to us humans. Humans are the only animals that create and use symbols.

When you think of Bigfoot, what comes to mind? Big feet, obviously, but also things like a huge size, long body hair, creepy glowing eyes, wood knocking and weird sounds, and threatening behavior, among other things. But what I saw there, carved into that tower, went way beyond all the stereotypes, for it indicated that whoever had made it was able to draw, to carve into wood, which meant they had opposable thumbs as well as a highly-developed brain.

It looked like a map. Maps are symbolic of the real landscape and exist to help one find their way. They are definitely considered to be symbols, though you don't often think of them like that.

I carry a little pocket camera, and I pulled it out and took a photo, which I still have. I then felt a strong and very urgent desire to obliterate the map, and I took my pocket knife and scratched it out until all that was left was the raw wood. Having done that, I felt a need to flee, and I took off down the trail at a half-run, suddenly feeling again like I was in danger, just like the previous night.

I ran until my side started aching, then I slowed to a fast walk, all the while my shotgun at hand. I never heard anything behind me, but yet I knew I needed to get down out of there.

Like I said earlier, the hike from Bowman Lake to the tower is around six miles, and I've never hiked six miles that fast before or since. Once at the lake's shore, I slowed to a normal pace out of necessity, as I was winded. It was early, but I could see a couple of people out on the lake in kayaks, and that made me feel like I was back to safety, so I caught my breath and took a short break. I was soon at the campground, where my pickup waited.

I never looked back, and I haven't been back since. I quit my work as a lookout and instead stayed at my girlfriend's place for a few weeks, then headed down to Missoula, where I found a job in a quick-lube place for the rest of the summer, saving my money by sleeping in my truck in the parking lot. I felt safer there in the middle of town than I had at the lookout tower, which was the opposite of what I would normally feel.

I finally went back to Kalispell and started working in a liquor store. My gal and I got married and started a lawn-care business, and in winters we go stay with my parents on the farm.

But in the summer, we like to go fishing on the Flathead River, and I can see those big peaks up in Glacier, peaks where I once lived. Sometimes I feel nostalgic for it, as it was a good life, but I know I can never go back after seeing that map.

I printed it out and studied it, and it still gives me the shakes, for there's no question about what it stands for, and I know these creatures aren't just intelligent, but are also very cunning, and they don't mean us any good.

What's the map all about? It has a rough sketch of the tower and a line going over to that meadow where we saw the two figures digging. I can still recall exactly where that meadow is, and I keep telling myself that someday I'm going to hike over there and see what's there, though I know I never will.

The map shows the meadow, and there, it has a sketch of what looks to be a human-like skull. It's almost as if someone had made that map to tell others where some kind of burial place was.

I have a lot of questions, though I know they'll never be answered. Did one of the creatures make that sketch to show the others where a burial site was? A number of people have gone missing in Glacier with no trace. Are they buried in that meadow or in similar ones in other places around the park? Was I destined to be placed there also?

It still gives me the chills. As far as I know, no lookout's gone missing from the Numa Ridge tower, but it's possible that a hiker or two has from that area. I guess I'd rather just not know.

6

THE IMAGINARY SASQUATCH

Alice and her two kids came along on one of my day-long fishing clinics on the Yellowstone River near Livingston, Montana, and it was really nice to see the three of them having so much fun, especially given that the kids were teens, who usually aren't that interested in fishing.

They were a really good-natured bunch, and when the kids laughingly told their mom to tell her Bigfoot story over our Dutch-oven dinner, I thought it was all a joke. But when she told her story, I knew it was as real as any I'd heard, and it makes me want to go visit the Two Medicine section of Glacier. —Rusty

I'm Alice, and this event happened one summer some 30 years ago when my little brother, Chuck, and I were camping with our mom and dad at Two Medicine in Glacier National Park. If you know the park, you'll know that the Two Medicine area is one of the quieter parts of Glacier, as it's on the east side of the park and harder to access from Kalispell.

We had a big cabin tent, the kind that would hold a half-dozen cots, and I remember it was a pain to set up, as it was heavy canvas. It didn't have a floor, which means all kinds of bugs and things could get in, but it was really watertight and kept us nice and dry, as it rained a lot while we were there.

We stayed at Two Medicine for two weeks, even though we'd planned on going to the other side of the park for one of those weeks. Dad had a two-week vacation, then we had to go back home to Rapid City.

Why did we spend an extra week at Two Medicine? I mean, we didn't even get to see the other side of the park, which we'd planned on doing, as we wanted to go camp over by Lake McDonald. All I can say was our plans were totally discombobulated by an event none of us could have predicted in a million years.

We had our dog, Jake, with us. He was quite the dog, medium-sized and kind of rangy, white with faint red spots, and the vet thought he was a Red Heeler mix. We got him from the shelter, though they called it the dog pound back then. He was very protective, yet liked everybody and was very gregarious. He also stayed close at hand, which is how working dogs are.

Back then, the park wasn't as strict as they are about dogs now, making you tie them all the time. Jake was a free-ranging dog, but he was good about sticking around. He'd always be on the lookout for squirrels and critters, kind of the self-imposed camp guard. He would patrol our camp, looking for trouble.

The park also wasn't as busy, and you never had a problem finding a campsite. There usually weren't all that many people around, which was nice.

Well, we'd been at Two Medicine for a couple of days, hiking and doing all the camping things that go with a summer vacation, having a great time. At night, we'd build a big fire and sit around talking, which was fun, as my mom knew a lot of good campfire stories, many revolving around bears or ghosts or things like that. I remember it was the first time I'd ever had a smore, which is a graham-cracker sandwich made with marshmallows and melted chocolate. I think I was around ten and Chuck was eight.

We had a big Coleman lantern that ran on white gas, and Dad would light that inside the tent after the fire went out so we could all see to get ready for bed. From outside, that big old cabin tent looked really eerie with that lantern glowing inside and shadowy figures moving around. I think Dad got both the lantern and the tent from some army-surplus place.

We sure didn't have the nice high-tech equipment campers have now, the sleek waterproof nylon tents with built-in pockets to store your clothes and with floors and sometimes even more than one room. But I will say our big old tent was sturdy and held up to high winds. It was kind of like sleeping outside, as you could hear everything going on around you.

Well, we'd been in Glacier almost a week when Jake came running into the tent where we were all sitting around a card table having sandwiches for lunch, as it was raining. He immediately ran and hid under one of the cots, shaking.

My mom jumped up and said, "I think there's a bear outside."

Dad also jumped up, and they both went outside, looking around, then came in and told us to get in the car. They'd heard something in the nearby bushes, and given how Jake was acting, they were taking no chances.

We actually had to put a leash on Jake and half-drag him to make him come out and go get in the car with us. My mom had grabbed all the sandwiches so the bear wouldn't get them, and we all sat in the car, eating, expecting to see a bear at any time. Jake was hiding down on the floor.

We tried to get him up on the seat, petting him and talking to him, but he wouldn't budge. We all remarked at how scared he was, as we'd never seen him act like that before. It was odd, because he was usually the first to go out and check if anything was amiss. We'd even seen him chase off a big bull one time when it had come into a meadow where we were camping in Idaho. But then, we weren't sure if he'd ever seen a bear.

Finally, after no sign of a bear, we all got out, and Jake decided everything was OK, as he followed us back into the tent, quiet, but acting more normal.

Since it was raining, we spent the rest of the day just hanging around camp, reading and playing card games. My little brother Chuck had decided he was going to turn into a mountain man, so he'd taken up whittling, trying to make a spear out of a stick he'd found. I guess the idea was to spear a fish if we all got hungry enough, which was unlikely, given how much food we'd brought.

Well, along about evening, Chuck decided he needed a better stick to whittle. He had a new plan—he would make a bow and some arrows, and that way he wouldn't have to get as close to his prey—he could hunt from afar. I guess he decided he would go after something bigger than a fish, maybe a rabbit or squirrel, not that mom would let him actually hunt anything, especially in a national park.

So, he and Jake went off into the nearby trees to find some appropriate sticks, though he was told to stay close. Growing up in the Black Hills of South Dakota, which has some really thick forests, we were all pretty savvy about how not to get lost in the woods, and he knew to not go far.

Well, it had only been a few minutes and here came Jake, running like the wind, heading straight for the tent, where he again hid. Chuck was close behind, and I could see he was about ready to cry as he, too, ran into the tent.

Well, we were soon all in the car again, including Jake, who Dad carried this time. Apparently Chuck had seen a bear, though he described it as a big hairy man. I've never seen him so scared, and he actually started crying, wanting to pack everything up and go home.

My parents patiently managed to get Chuck to tell his story, even though they knew it had to have been a bear. But what Chuck told us was pretty scary, and I remember also wanting to pack up and leave, just like Chuck had said we should.

He said he'd been only about 50 feet back in the trees, looking for sticks, when Jake had suddenly turned and ran away, which was so unlike him that Chuck stood there for a moment before it registered that something dangerous must be nearby.

He said he suddenly felt more scared than he'd ever been in his short life, and as he turned to follow Jake, he saw a large hairy man standing nearby, holding something that looked like a young gorilla.

The thing made a purring type noise, holding out the little gorilla like it wanted Chuck to take it.

As mom and dad talked to him, trying to figure it all out, Chuck decided the small gorilla was maybe the child of the large hairy man, which he then decided was a woman, for when it held the younger one out away from it, he could see it had breasts. He said the creature started making a soft noise as if it were crying, and he was overcome with a sadness that made him want to stop and help it, but he was too scared.

Now, let me add a little here about Chuck—he was famous for having an overactive imagination. Just about every time he was out after dark, he'd come back inside with stories about UFOs and how they'd tried to get him to go up with them, or even how he *had* actually gone up with them. He would describe how things looked from high above, and he usually sounded very convincing. At one point he had an imaginary friend he named Doo-Dah, which was pretty amusing, and he and Doo-Dah were always having grand adventures. After reading a book on the Ice Age, he got good at seeing Pleistocene animals around, things like dire bears and dire wolves. He said he actually befriended a mammoth at one point, and then after that it all segued into dinosaurs. Then one day, after we'd eaten at an Italian restaurant, he had a friend named Pasta for a few months.

Well, you get the idea. You'd think that with an imagination like that, he would've grown up to be a filmmaker or writer or something, but instead he became a mechanic. But I will say that his outlandish stories really took a hit after this happened. I think he finally realized what it would be like if his stories were real, and it scared him.

Well, after awhile, I could tell Mom and Dad didn't really believe him, though they were being very kind and tried to make him understand that such things just didn't exist. But somehow this time felt different, for Chuck didn't usually get emotional when telling his wild tales. Plus, it was kind of hard to explain why Jake was acting so strange.

Well, we left Jake in the car, and Mom and Dad persuaded Chuck to go show them where he'd seen this creature, even though he didn't want to. I didn't want to go, though I didn't really believe the story, so I told them I would stay in the car with Jake, since someone should be around to go get the ranger in case everyone disappeared.

But Mom made me come along, and I think we were all pretty much convinced he'd seen a bear, if anything, and Dad had his bear spray handy.

Later, Mom and Dad said they knew it was probably foolish to go back into the woods, given that Chuck may have actually seen a bear, but his story was so outlandish that they didn't think he'd really seen anything at all and had made it all up.

So, we all carefully walked back to where he'd seen this thing, which wasn't far from camp at all, in fact, I could still see the sun shining off the car bumper. But Chuck was now acting as if he was about to cry again, so I guess my parents decided we'd gone far enough. It was then that I noticed something dark brown over in the bushes. At that point, I was too scared to say anything, so I just tugged on my mom's sleeve and pointed.

"It's a cub!" She said. "We need to get out of here before the mom comes back."

We went back to the car, and once safely inside, a debate started —should they go back and see if the cub was OK, or just get a ranger?

It ended up with my dad deciding to go take a quick look, and if the cub was still there and looked like it might be injured or something, they'd get a ranger. He knew it was a risky thing to do, but he had his bear spray, and it was so close to camp we couldn't just ignore it.

Well, Chuck and I didn't know for years what actually happened out there, as my dad wouldn't tell us, though I know he told my mom. But he was gone long enough that we started to get really worried, and when he showed back up, he was white as a ghost and very quiet.

He took my mom into the tent to talk, telling us to stay in the car, and when they came back out, they had the first-aid kit. Now my mom also looked as white as a ghost. They told us to stay put, and if they weren't back in a half-hour, to go get a ranger, but under no circumstance were we to come into the woods looking for them.

It was all very strange and mysterious.

I'll never forget sitting in that car in the campground at Two Medicine with Chuck, wondering what was going on and if we would ever see our parents again.

Chuck started crying again, and I asked him to describe in detail what he'd seen, thinking it might help him get over it, but he didn't want to talk about it any more. Like I said, it was the beginning of the end of his wild stories, which was kind of sad in a way, because he was always very entertaining, but this one seemed to knock the stuffing out of him.

So, we waited in the car. At one point, we heard a strange cry, and this made us both really worried, but fortunately our parents returned soon after. They both looked relieved, and we were allowed to get out of the car, though they told us Jake had to stay on a leash from then on, and we were not to even think about going anywhere out of their sight.

There was talk of moving camp, but in the end, they decided to stay, saying they didn't want anyone else to find the "cub," which was injured. They'd tried to help it as best they could.

We were going to stay there as long as it took to make sure the cub was OK, and Chuck and I were not to go near it, as the mom could be very dangerous. And from then on, Chuck and I were to sleep in the car with Jake, where it was safer.

It was all very secretive, and after that, our vacation went from being fun to being tense and on edge. I wondered why they didn't just get a ranger, as we'd been told since we were little that you didn't mess with wildlife—and yet, here they were, doing exactly that.

Our first night in the car was terrifying, to say the least. We had strict orders to not get out for any reason, and if we needed to go to the bathroom, we were to yell for one of our parents—and we had to keep the doors locked.

Later, Mom and Dad said they hadn't wanted for us to know exactly what was going on because they knew we'd be afraid, but in retrospect, I think it would've been better if they'd been straight up with us from the start. After all, Chuck had already seen the thing, and he knew what was going on to some extent. Leaving us in the dark made things much worse, given what kids' imaginations can do, especially Chuck's.

So, that first night in the car, we hunkered down in our sleeping bags, Chuck in the front and me in the back with Jake, wondering what was out there in the dark and if our parents would survive the night with only a canvas tent for safety.

It didn't help things when we heard a crying sound coming from the direction where the cub was. It was loud enough that we knew it wasn't the cub, but was instead probably its mom crying her heart out.

Later, when it was all said and done and Mom and Dad would talk about things, we found out it wasn't a bear cub at all, but was what Dad called a Sasquatch. He refused to call it a Bigfoot, saying the term was derogatory and made it sound silly, like something with huge feet from a cartoon. He always called it a Sasquatch cub.

Later, we learned that when Dad had first gone into the woods to look at the cub, he could see it had been put in a small nest made of sticks and soft grasses. He said it was in obvious pain and was very still, kind of like a young fawn or something would be, knowing that it should be quiet so as to not attract predators.

Dad was scared to death, but he managed to get close enough to it to see it had a small branch run almost all the way through its foot. And to make things worse, the stick was flush with the foot, as if someone had tried to extract it and had instead broken it off. It was quite a mess, he said. All he could figure was that the cub had jumped off something and hit the stick, the impact running it into its foot. He was afraid to touch it, yet knew it needed help. And all the while he was there, he was aware that something was watching him, but he didn't feel threatened, but instead that it badly wanted him to fix it.

He went back and got my mom, not really sure what to do. Should he call a ranger? What would they do with it? Or maybe there was a vet in Browning, which was the nearest town.

He and Mom talked about it for awhile, then decided to try to help the cub as best they could and take it from there. Now, my parents weren't doctors or nurses, but they both had been around animals a lot, both having grown up on farms, and they kind of knew the basics.

Mom said it was really harrowing when they first touched the cub, as they had no idea if its mom would attack them or if the cub would fight. But the cub was very docile, being in a lot of pain, and they never saw the mom. They knew she was nearby and aware of what they were doing.

The wound was starting to fester, and Mom gave the cub some pain killers she had for emergencies, though she and dad had wondered if it would be safe to do so. I guess she just stuck them in its mouth and it ate them or something.

After awhile, the cub went to sleep, and they were able to pull the stick out with some needle-nose pliers Dad had. They then poured antiseptic onto the wound. When they left, the cub was still sleeping, and Mom was worried they'd given it something that wasn't good for it. They could hear a purring noise coming from the bushes, and they figured it was its mom.

We spent the next few days in camp, our parents going to check on the so-called cub every day, putting more antiseptic on the wound. The mom was apparently feeding it, as when they took it some biscuits, it didn't want them. They left them for the mom, and they were gone next time they went out there, so they started taking left-overs out for her, as they figured she wasn't able to forage or hunt much while watching over the cub.

Between these nursing sessions, we'd go for hikes around the lake and play games and do stuff like that, but in all honesty, Chuck and I just wanted to go home. We were scared sleeping in the car like that, though we were starting to get used to it. And poor Jake! He was used to running free and suddenly had to be on a leash, which he didn't like one bit.

At that time, you could stay in the campground at Two Medicine for two weeks max, and our time was almost up. We would have to leave, regardless of how the cub was doing, though Mom said its foot seemed to be healing well.

A couple of days before we would have to leave, Chuck and I were awakened at dawn by Jake's growling. He then tried to get under my sleeping bag, which was impossible since I was still in it.

I knew there was something in camp, and as I leaned up on my elbow, I could see a large black creature by the picnic table. It was still almost dark, so I didn't get a good look, but I did see enough to know it wasn't a bear.

It looked over my way, maybe aware of motion in the car, then quickly slipped into the woods and was gone. I felt scared and confused, too afraid to even roll the window down and wake my parents, and I gradually slipped back asleep.

When I woke, I could smell something really good cooking, something different. Mom and Dad had breakfast ready, and Chuck and Jake were already up. Mom told us to pack all our stuff when we were done eating, as we were going home.

She said that when they'd gone out to check on the cub that morning, it was gone, and they knew it was now able to walk, its wound healed.

The smell was the most delicious rainbow trout I'd ever had, and along with some fried potatoes, it was a delicious breakfast. I can still smell it when I think of that morning on the shore of Two Medicine Lake.

Had Dad gone fishing before we got up? It wasn't at all like him, for he wasn't much of a fisherman, nor an early riser. When I asked, Mom said that someone had left a big beautiful trout on the picnic table. She had no idea who, but wondered if it wasn't maybe the neighbors, who had already left for the day.

When I told her what I'd seen, she got real quiet, then told Dad, who just smiled, saying it was a gift.

We were soon packed and gone, and though I've been back to Glacier several times, I've never returned to Two Medicine. I guess the memory of what happened is still with me enough that I feel a bit of anxiety when I think of it, but since my kids are wanting to go, I know that one of these days I'll have to buckle down and face my fears from long-ago.

I often think of that Sasquatch "cub" my parents helped and hope it's OK. It's probably a big strapping Sasquatch at this point, or at least so I hope. When I asked them years later what it looked like, they said it was just like Chuck had told us, like a baby gorilla. I'll never know why they never took any pictures of it, but knowing my dad, it was probably from respect for the mom, or even fear, for he knew she was watching.

My parents have been gone for a number of years, and after they told Chuck and me what had happened, they never talked about it again. To this day, Chuck won't talk about it, saying it was all a figment of our imaginations, that we'd all had too much sun, even though it rained most of the time we were there. I find this ironic, given all the tall tales he used to tell, swearing they were true, but he always swore that the Sasquatch cub was imaginary.

But when I ask him if he remembers how good that imaginary trout given to us by the imaginary Sasquatch tasted, he always says it was the best trout he's ever imagined eating.

7

TROUBLE AT THE PTARMIGAN TUNNEL

I met Ranger Chris at the Black Canyon. It's a national park not too far from where I live in Steamboat Springs, Colorado, and I was there with a couple of friends on what turned out to be a big fishing boondoggle.

Chris was very helpful, telling us about a good fishing spot that was actually accessible and not 2,000 feet straight down, and when we got to talking, I learned he was a fisherman, too, and invited him to come up to my stomping grounds. He actually did come up, and his visit was very enjoyable, but I will say it turned more to the dark side when he told me the following story. —Rusty

W ell, Rusty, so we meet again. I really enjoyed talking with you at the Black Canyon, and I hate to say it, but your buddy wasn't the first fisherman to not read the maps right. At least you guys didn't actually try to get down to the river. It can be done from Gunnison Point, but I've been on more than one rescue party that involved fishermen in that canyon.

Anyway, I don't remember how we got to talking about Glacier National Park, but I've thought a lot about it since our conversation. I have to admit that, even though I agree with you that it's a stunningly beautiful place, it's one park I'll probably never visit again.

I was a park ranger up there for 15 years and left under what some of my fellow rangers called questionable circumstances. I got transferred, first to Badlands National Park, then to the Black Canyon, where I hope to stay until I retire.

I know Glacier well—all too well, I should say. Sometimes I really miss it, it's so rugged and wild, but when I think about what happened there, I'm glad I'm gone. I will say I don't miss the winters, beautiful as they are. And I like driving home each night to my house in the middle of pastoral farmland, as opposed to where I lived in West Glacier, surrounded by wildlands.

But before I get started, I want to say that my story isn't the only one like it. Afterwards, when I finally opened up and started talking to some of my more trusted coworkers, I found that some of them had had similar experiences or knew someone who had. And I wasn't the first to transfer out of there.

Let me add that I don't understand why the topic of Bigfoot is so taboo to so many people. It's almost like you're saying you're superstitious or ignorant to believe in them, which I don't think is the case. Sure, we have no hard evidence of them, at least not the kind that goes into a lab or museum or such, but that doesn't mean they don't exist.

I think that if people were more open about the topic, it would be surprising how many have seen them. I know I have, and so have at least a half-dozen of my friends up at Glacier. Sometimes it's better to know about things so you can be forewarned. I wish I'd been.

Anyway, as to where this all happened, it was near one of the more popular places in Glacier, in the Many Glacier region. It's a beautiful area with lots of hiking trails, as well as picturesque glacial lakes and mountains. It also has lots of amenities, such as the historic Many Glacier Lodge and several restaurants and such, which help draw people there.

One accesses Many Glacier by going across Logan Pass on the Going to the Sun Road, or you can also drive around the south side of the park. The Many Glacier Valley is a huge U-shaped valley surrounded by horns and sharp mountain ridges, all carved by the huge glaciers of long ago, some of which were more than a mile thick.

One of the hallmarks of all this glacial activity are the arêtes, which are basically sharp spines ground by huge glaciers on each side. A lot of people are familiar with the Garden Wall, a huge arête that separates the McDonald Valley from the Many Glacier Valley, but another big arête is the Ptarmigan Wall, which separates the Many Glacier Valley from the Belly River Valley.

If you've ever hiked to the famous Iceberg Lake, you've been right under the Ptarmigan Wall. In fact, you've even hiked part of the trail that my Bigfoot encounter happened on, because the Iceberg Lake Trail and the Ptarmigan Trail start out in the same place, then diverge after a few miles.

As a ranger, I knew the Ptarmigan Wall well, for one of my jobs was to go open the Ptarmigan Tunnel each summer when the snows melted enough to hike the trail. The tunnel was built in the 1930s by the CCC, the Civilian Conservation Corps, and it was quite an accomplishment, especially for its time. It's 250 feet long and cuts straight through the arête, making the Belly River side accessible from the Many Glacier side, whereas you once had to hike over Redgap Pass.

It took three months to blast out the tunnel, two jack-hammer drillers coming from each side and meeting in the middle. They also used rounds of dynamite. The tunnel was originally intended for horseback riders to connect with chalets throughout the park. Now that most of the chalets are gone, it serves hikers and backpackers.

Since the tunnel is where I had my encounter, maybe I should describe it some. Each portal of the tunnel has a wide area with a retaining wall overlooking the valley, originally made as a place for the guide and tourists and their horses to hang out. The interior walls of the tunnel are lined with the original rock, and you can see where it was all jack-hammered.

In 1975, heavy iron doors were hung across the tunnel adits, or openings. We typically close them on October 1, sometimes earlier.

The main purpose of the doors is to keep the tunnel from filling with snow, but they give the tunnel a fortress-like feel.

I know my ranger background is showing, but I think some of this is important to the setting and to understanding my encounter. It's definitely a unique place, and the roughage from the tunnel itself was used to build low rock walls along the upper part of the trail on both sides, as it's hairy, with lots of exposure. Even with the walls, it's very exposed feeling.

The views are simply breathtaking. On the south side, you look down on Ptarmigan Lake, and on the north, you have staggering views into the Belly River drainage.

Sadly enough, in 1998, a Montana woman lost her life in one of the most freakish accidents in Glacier National Park history. A group led their horses through the tunnel to the other side, and there, the woman's horse stumbled, knocking her onto the retaining wall, then falling on top of her. Both then rolled over the wall before falling 1,400 feet to their deaths. So, as you can see, it can be a dangerous place.

Anyway, it was my job to hike to the tunnel and determine when the trail was accessible enough to open it. Typically, because it's so high up, the tunnel isn't opened until mid-July, and sometimes even later in big snow years.

OK, enough background. On to what actually happened up there, a place I once loved but that will never feel the same to me again.

I remember the day well—it was July 12th. I got my daypack ready, told everyone where I was going, then headed out. There have been years when the tunnel was accessible in early July, and it hadn't been a record snow year, so I actually wasn't too far off on my timing. In fact, the tunnel was accessible, as I found out, even though the trail was still somewhat snowy.

Now, since I've probably bored you to death with all these details about the tunnel, let me tell you about the trail. A lot of it goes through prime huckleberry bushes, so we tell everyone to carry bear spray, as it's a very popular area for bears, especially black bears. In fact, we often close the trail down in the late summer when the huck-leberries are ripe, there are so many bears.

I've had lots of people come back all excited, wanting to report a bear sighting along this trail. Remember, it's also the trail to Iceberg Lake at the beginning, which is possibly the most popular trail in the Many Glacier region. There are signs everywhere telling people it's a popular bear area and to be bear aware. But I've had a few who told me they saw something that was definitely not a bear.

Well, it's also a popular area for moose. Moose are large animals, and if you only see part of one in the shrubs, it's easy to think you've seen something really big, because you have. Most people mistake them for bears until they can see more of the animal. So, when people tell me they saw something large that wasn't a bear, I gener-ally think they've seen a moose. I know it's kind of circular, but given the fact that the majority of tourists know nothing about nature, they often make identification mistakes.

But there are also hikers out there who are more trail savvy, and I tend to listen more carefully when they tell me stuff, because they usually have the experience to know what they're talking about. Over the years, I've heard a few really hairy stories from such people coming from the area of the tunnel and the Belly River Valley.

Okay, I made a little joke on myself by saying hairy stories, and you can guess what I'm talking about—it's sure not bears. The stories would be about being stalked and menaced and things like that, and there never was a report of any actual harm, but whatever was up there sure liked to scare people.

I have to admit hearing these stories would freak me out for some time afterwards, but I usually felt they were just a product of overac-tive imaginations, even though most people were pretty convincing.

So, that day in July, I headed up the trail, along with a number of other hikers, all who seemed to be going to Iceberg Lake, since the tunnel was closed. Part of the attraction of going to the tunnel was being able to walk through it and see the view out the other side, so few people went up there when it was closed.

I parted ways with the Iceberg Lake Trail above Ptarmigan Falls and began following Ptarmigan Creek, the knife-edge of the Ptarmigan Wall dominating my view. I was now alone, everyone else having taken the trail to Iceberg. The trail was now fairly steep, going through a thick patch of huckleberry bushes, an area where I would see a bear every single time I hiked through there.

My bear spray handy, I made lots of noise and soon climbed above treeline, the view of the Ptarmigan Wall even more dramatic, towering more than 1,700 feet above the trail at this point. The lower saddle on the wall where the tunnel went through was now directly in my line of sight.

I stopped, taking a break to sit on a rock and drink some water and eat a sandwich from my pack. It was the first time I hadn't seen a bear at some point along the trail, which was surprising, though not overly so, as the berries weren't yet ripe. But the area was also full of glacier lilies, which bears loved.

As I sat there, I realized I hadn't seen any wildlife at all—not one single moose or elk or deer or even a marmot. Had I seen any birds? I didn't recall seeing any, but then, I was distracted and not really watching for them. But I think that what I saw later had a lot to do with the wildlife being scarce.

I was soon back on the trail, passing a series of waterfalls and cascades tumbling down into the valley below, now above Ptarmigan Lake. I got out my little camera, as bighorn sheep and mountain goats frequented this area, as well as the area above the two major switch-backs climbing to the tunnel.

The trail now became steep, gaining around 500 feet in less than two-thirds of a mile. I had to take it slow, even though I was anxious to enjoy the spectacular views that I knew awaited me on the other side of the tunnel.

So far, there had been snow only in a few shady places along the trail, but now an inch or so covered everything, getting a little deeper as I climbed, though it didn't look like it would get deep enough to prevent me from opening the tunnel. I was somewhat surprised to see no animal tracks, so I figured it must be fresh snow.

I finally put my camera away, as there wasn't a goat or sheep in sight anywhere, which was unusual. Usually, at least a few goats could be seen high on the cliffs above, their white coats making them easy to spot.

As I reached the second switchback, I turned to enjoy the views behind me of Ptarmigan Lake far below, with Mt. Wilbur dominating the skyline. A feeling of elation hit me, and I was glad to be in the high country again. Being a park ranger definitely has its ups and downs, and this was for sure one of the ups.

But as I turned back towards the tunnel, a feeling of uneasiness hit me like a ton of bricks from nowhere. I looked all around to see if maybe there was a grizzly nearby, since my intuition was on red alert, but I saw nothing.

I scanned the trail ahead, and I could make out what looked like tracks coming down. Someone must've come from the other side of the tunnel, opening the doors and coming on through. But why didn't they continue on down?

It looked like they'd turned back, which seemed strange. Maybe someone had come from the Belly River side and then gone back the same way, though that didn't make sense, for a backpacker would be wanting to get to Many Glacier after such a long hike.

When I reached the tracks, the snow was a good three or four inches deep, enough to easily see the prints. It was puzzling, because they didn't look like a bear's or a human's, but rather like someone wearing flat-soled overshoes, but with their toes sticking out. I examined them for a long time, trying to figure them out, and the longer I knelt there, the stranger things began to feel.

I did take some photos, and I still have them, but I've never shown them to anyone except a couple of close friends. It was a bright sunny day, and unfortunately a lot of the detail is washed out.

What was really strange was when I realized the tracks didn't come from the tunnel, but instead came straight down off the Ptarmigan Wall, which would be pretty much an impossibility unless you were a monkey. The wall's made of sedimentary layers, and most humans would need technical gear to climb it. I say most because I know of a few free climbers who might be able to do it, but it would be very dangerous. The other side is just as bad.

I decided the tracks must be partially melted to look like that, as well as the bear overstepping with its back feet, which was common. I've seen lots of bear tracks that looked really odd because of the hind feet stepping into the front tracks. But what bothered me most was that the tracks looked so fresh.

In retrospect, I should've listened to my heart, as it was pounding, telling me to turn around and go back. I wrote it off as being out of shape, which I actually wasn't. I'd been hiking the trails in the park since they opened in the summer, and before that, snowshoeing and skiing all winter.

The other thing that bothered me was that the tracks didn't sink in nearly as far as their size would suggest they should. I mean, these tracks were easily twice the size of my size 10, yet they didn't sink in as far as mine did. I finally decided the snow must've been more frozen when they were made, but later, after what I saw and after thinking about it, I wondered if whatever made them was very lightweight.

Well, the tracks came down from the wall and then up to the tunnel. Whatever had made them was either waiting at the portal, assuming the doors were still closed, or had gone on through and out the other side.

I got out my binoculars and scanned the mountainside, seeing nothing unusual, then found the door to the tunnel, which was still far enough away that it looked like a small hole to the unaided eye. But with the binoculars, I could see a blackness that told me the door was open, as otherwise I'd be seeing the silver metal doors. I could make out the shiny metal frame, but no door, just a black hole.

OK, the door was open. I might as well turn around and go back, no need to continue. Basically, all we would do is open the doors and prop them with rocks so they would stay open, then go home, job done.

But I've always been pretty conscientious, so, even though I felt hesitant, I decided to go on up and make sure everything was as it should be. I was almost up there anyway, just another 30 minutes or so away. Besides, I wanted to get some good photos from the other portal of the Belly River Valley. So, I kept hiking. I know now I shouldn't have.

OK, now things get really strange. I was maybe all of a quarter mile from the tunnel when the tracks disappeared into thin air. They turned as if going right up the rock wall and disappeared. I stopped and once again got out my binoculars, scanning the cliff walls above me, but saw nothing. I did smell a faint odor, though, which seemed really out of place since it smelled like a mix between gunpowder and something dead. I know that's odd, but it's exactly what it was like.

Now I was really puzzled. My gut was telling me to get out of there ASAP, but my sense of wanting to finish the job was strong. I was so close—I would just hurry to the tunnel, check on things, then head back.

The snow was deeper now since I was gaining altitude, maybe five or six inches at that point, but not enough to keep the tunnel closed. I made my way up to the portal as quickly as possible, and sure enough, the doors were open. I'm not sure, but I think maybe the park locks the doors now, but back then, they were just pushed shut.

I pushed the doors all the way open, propped them with a couple of big rocks that were there for that purpose, then entered the tunnel. I could see a dim light ahead, telling me the other door was also open. At that point, I figured some hiker had come through, his tracks covered with the recent snow, and the bear or whatever had come through later.

The inside of the Ptarmigan Tunnel is very closed-in feeling, and I have a touch of claustrophobia anyway, so I went through as quickly as possible, almost jogging. Just as I reached the far door, I heard an awful clanging sound. Turning, I realized someone had slammed the big double doors shut, someone with a lot of strength, for they're not light. It's hard to close them, yet alone make them clang.

I stood in shock for a moment, trying to understand what had just happened, and more importantly, why. It didn't make sense for someone to shut the doors. Were they now inside or outside the tunnel? And where in heck had they come from? I'd stopped enough to look around coming up that I knew there was no one behind me. Could they have been hiding in the cliffs above? If so, they were more agile than I was, by far.

I quickly reached the far door and slipped outside, glad to be free from the darkness and smell of damp rock. I stopped for a moment at the portal, the red sedimentary layers of Crowfoot Mountain to my right, almost dazzling in the bright sunlight. I could see the blue of Elizabeth Lake far below.

I didn't tarry, again wondering who'd slammed the door. If they were in the tunnel, they would soon reach my side, and I wasn't so sure it was anyone I wanted to meet. It might be prudent to make myself scarce, at least until I could see who it was and assess the situation.

I wasn't a law-enforcement ranger, so the only protection I carried was bear spray. Because I was unarmed, I always erred on the side of prudence, trying to be situationally aware, and I knew I needed to get out of there.

The only problem was, there was no place to go. Like the other side of the arête, this side was straight up, though it did have a number of jagged protrusions and shelves, but none I was capable of climbing. The trail headed across the flank of Crowfoot Mountain, going straight-shot for a long ways until it disappeared around the distant mountainside, heading for Redgap Pass. There was a stand of trees about midway down, but it was a long ways off.

I only stood there for a moment, then I panicked. Something told me that door hadn't been slammed by some hiker messing around, but was meant to entrap me. I needed to hide, and soon.

I took off running. I had no idea if I was actually in any kind of danger, and I really wasn't prepared to hike the miles it would take me to get back to Many Glacier by going over Redgap Pass, so why did I panic like that? All I can say is that it was intuition.

I think that the only thing that saved me was the fact that the trail didn't take off straight across the flank of Crowfoot Mountain, but instead angled around a break in the mountainside and was hidden from the tunnel for a short distance. I know whatever this thing was didn't see me, and it's a good thing, for I don't think I would've had much of a chance if it had, and it seemed like it was definitely after me.

How do I know that? First, when it emerged from the tunnel, it let out a bellow that sounded angry and malevolent, making me very glad I hadn't waited around. It then began shrieking, and even though I couldn't see it, I knew it had to be large to have that kind of lung power.

There I was, running down that trail for all I was worth, even though I had no idea what was behind me. My gut said I was in terrible danger, and I have no idea why it didn't see me. Maybe it was looking up, thinking I'd scaled the cliffs.

I finally reached the stand of trees and stopped. I had no choice, as my side was aching and I was out of breath. I had to look back, to see if it was coming after me, so I carefully peeked out where I knew it couldn't see me.

There was nothing there, which made me very happy, though I was still wary. But suddenly, movement caught my eye. Something white was climbing straight up the wall above the tunnel door! I took out my binoculars, and I kind of wish I hadn't, for what I saw gave me chills.

It was tall and thin, wiry, even, and though I was now some distance away, I had good binoculars and was able to make out enough to leave me terrified. It looked like a tall thin gorilla, except its face was more like a human's, though I couldn't see it all that well. It was tremendously hairy, long waves hanging from its arms, and it was incredibly agile. It quickly scaled the rocks and was gone before I could even process what I was seeing. I knew it had been above me on the trail, but I hadn't seen it because it blended in with the white snowy slope.

I turned and continued down the trail. There was no way I was going back through the tunnel. Fortunately, I was very familiar with the park, being a ranger, and I knew I could get back to Many Glacier via Redgap Pass, though it would be a long slog of many miles, yet vastly preferable to being ambushed at the Ptarmigan Tunnel.

I've thought about this many times, about how that huge creature could scale those cliffs so easily, and I have a theory.

When I lived in West Glacier, I had a big tree in my front yard, a 100-year old pine. I had trimmed the branches on it about eight-feet up so I could get under it to rake the pine needles and such. That tree had a family of squirrels living in it, and every so often I would throw out a handful of nuts or some dried apples for them.

When I saw that white creature climbing that steep wall, it reminded my of those squirrels. It just went straight up, using all four limbs, like a squirrel climbs a tree. You wonder what they're holding on with.

After seeing that, I now believe that some Bigfoot are very lightweight creatures, in fact, maybe Glacier has a subspecies that's lightweight and also white. These particular Bigfoot must have very light bones. Watch one climb sometime, and you'll agree with me (though hopefully you'll never see one).

How could they be so lightweight? If you read about birds, you'll find that they have very light bones that are hollow and filled with air. This allows them to fly. Interestingly enough, paleontologists have wondered for a long time how some dinosaurs could grow to be so large, especially the big vegetation-eating monsters. These things were so huge that it seemed like gravity would weigh them down to where they couldn't even walk.

But now that they know that birds evolved from some types of dinosaurs, they now believe that these big giants also had hollow bones and didn't weigh nearly what one would think. They were actually pretty lightweight and could run faster than one might guess.

Anyway, watching that thing scale that steep spine was really mind boggling, I can tell you. I felt like I was watching a movie, it seemed so surreal. And yet, I knew it could soon be down to where I was, and I didn't have much time to act, so I basically began running again. It was difficult reconciling the grip of fantasy with the necessity of saving oneself, I can tell you.

My trek out was, in itself, pretty harrowing, as I kept hearing and imagining things behind me, especially after it got dark. I was prepared and had a good headlamp, plus I'd hiked Redgap Pass before, so knew what to expect, but it was still quite an adventure, one I would've preferred to not have.

I took the next day off, exhausted, still trying to process what I'd seen. I had no idea what to do—should I go back up with someone else and make sure the tunnel was open, or should I tell my boss everything that had happened and face possible ridicule?

The next evening, after I was more rested, I called my good friend Cindy, who worked at the Many Glacier Lodge, and asked her to come over. We talked late into the night, and I still wasn't sure what to do. She said I would be ridiculed and not believed, which I knew was true, but how could I let hikers possibly walk right into the same danger I had? And yet, how could I warn them if nobody believed me? And what exactly could the park do, anyway?

It was a quandary, and when I went back to work the next day, I decided that honesty was the best policy, as they say. I told my supervisor all about my experience. He was a seasoned ranger and had been with the park service his entire career, knowing how things worked, and he didn't even know where to begin with all this.

He basically asked if I wanted to transfer out, and he didn't seem surprised when I immediately said yes, even though I hadn't even had time to think about it. I didn't need to think about it, I guess, for as much as I loved Glacier, I knew I could never be comfortable out in the wilds, especially alone, which was basically my job. I got the feeling he believed me, though he said nothing.

At my going away party, he wished me well, saying he'd given me a sterling reference. I was going to Badlands National Park, far from the wilds of Glacier and its strange creatures.

But I'll never forget his final words to me that night, which I'll paraphrase as best I can.

"Chris, you know that my official stance has to be that what you saw doesn't exist. But you're the third ranger that's left on these grounds since I started working here, and I know you're not *all* hallucinating. I really don't want to see one, but if I ever do, I'll get in touch. In the meantime, have a great time at Badlands."

Rusty, I'll never forget his words, because two years later to the day, he disappeared in the backcountry not far from the Ptarmigan Tunnel and was never found. I often wonder if he didn't meet up with that creature in a most unfortunate way.

I badly wanted to go help look for him and tried to get the time off, but we were too busy, and the park guys in Glacier said they had lots of search and rescue people out looking, so I didn't go. I was actually glad to hear I wasn't really needed, as deep inside, I didn't want to go back.

In a way, I'm glad I stayed home, for who knows—maybe I wouldn't have come back. No point in tempting Fate twice, I guess—or maybe I should say, no point in tempting *Bigfoot* twice.

8

THE HAND

Sometimes, when I look through all the Bigfoot stories I've collected, I wonder if it could really be possible for that many people to have seen these creatures. But when I go online and look at some of the Bigfoot sites and forums, I realize that my collection is actually pretty small in comparison to what's out there.

I've never actually counted all the encounters I've recorded, and many of them don't really merit retelling, as they're of the variety of "we saw a Bigfoot cross the road," but some are real humdingers. These are the ones I try to get more of the story, to learn about the people involved, their lives and feelings and all that. And I will say that sometimes I'm actually shocked by what people have seen and gone through.

This following story came from a fellow who was on one of my guided trips on the Yellowstone. When I first heard it, it seemed surreal, but he was very straightforward and swore it actually happened. When I contacted his friend, Al, who was also there, his version matched perfectly, down to the most minute details. I was kind of hoping it wasn't true, for this is a side of Bigfoot we all hope to never meet. —Rusty

. . .

R usty, I'm Dave, and my friend Al accompanied me on this trip. I can put you in touch with him to verify the details of this story. Even though it happened a few years back, it's still very fresh in my memory.

I've read a number of Bigfoot accounts since this happened, and I've noticed that most people who had an encounter had no idea what was coming. A lot of people were surprised by what they saw, but that simply wasn't the case with us. We had plenty of warning, and yet we chose to disregard the signs and indications of trouble.

Why would we do this? In retrospect, I'm not sure, except to say we were clueless. Bigfoot wasn't even on our radar, and at the time, we found all kinds of ways to discount what we were hearing and seeing, at least until it became so obvious that we finally had no choice but to wake up. When we did, it was shocking. I guess that's how we humans tend to be—we're in denial until we have to accept something.

Al and I were good friends—actually, we still are, even though this incident stretched our comfort zones with one another some. At the time, we were both working as wedding photographers in Jackson, Wyoming, which can be a pretty lucrative business in a resort town like that, for lots of people want to be married with the beautiful Tetons in the background.

Photography can be a tough business, primarily because everyone thinks they're a photographer, especially with the availability of good inexpensive gear these days. Heck, you can now take photos with cell phones that would put many professionals to shame. Because of this, it's hard to make a living anymore doing stock photography, so lots of photographers have switched to shooting weddings, even though they'd prefer to be landscape or wildlife photographers. That's exactly how it was with us.

Al and I go way back, clear to high school in the little town of Pinedale, Wyoming. We became friends in our high-school photography club, and even though we both went our separate ways after graduation, we met up again in Jackson at a workshop given by a famous wildlife photographer there.

At that point, we were both married and working jobs we hated. We decided to pool our money and do some marketing, and for some reason, our business really took off. We became the go-to people in that area for wedding photography.

Wedding photography is typically hectic and stressful. You don't get a second chance on shots, and they'd better be good, for you're recording a once in a lifetime event. We worked well as a team, and Al would take videos while I did the stills. So, we were used to working under pressure.

Well, the autumn this happened, we'd been working hard all summer, making good money, but we were exhausted, and we decided we needed a break. Our hearts have always been in land-scape and wildlife photography, so we talked about it, and decided to go on up to Glacier National Park for two weeks.

Since it was late September, we knew the park visitation would be slowing, with most tourists gone. We could do some nice day-hikes and hopefully get some good photos of the autumn colors, as well as maybe film a few bears before they went into hibernation.

The plan was to rent something near Glacier, which would mean we could have the comforts of home and yet get going really early and take hikes to where we wanted to be each day. If you want good landscape shots, you need to get out before sunrise so you can be where you want when the sun actually comes up. Early mornings were also the best time for wildlife shots.

So, we rented a place for a week near West Glacier, the west entrance to the park. We then rented a small cabin at Many Glacier for the second week, over on the other side of the park. Neither were fancy or anything, since all we really wanted was a place to sleep. We hoped to be out and about every day making photos.

We were excited, as we'd been talking about maybe putting together some coffee table books or a calendar, and we knew from friends that anything to do with Glacier usually sold well. Our conversation on the way up there from Jackson was mostly about how we were going to use this as a springboard to get us out of the wedding business. We were both Wyoming boys, and to be honest, it was our nature to be solitary. That's why we'd chosen photography in the first place.

Well, going to Glacier was just what the doctor ordered, and I will say our first week was fantastic. We spent time on the shores of Lake McDonald, which is one of the most photographed places in Glacier, and for good reason. We ventured up to Bowman and Kintla lakes in the North Fork region, with good results there, also.

But a few days after we arrived, something strange happened. We'd hiked up to Avalanche Lake, a popular spot not far from the Avalanche Campground. We had set up our cameras by the lower part of the lake when a group of hikers came by.

They stopped, all excited, telling us we should pack up and get out. When we finally got them slowed down enough to make sense, they told us they'd been up at the top of the lake, just below the head-wall of the valley, when they'd heard a strange howling coming from high above.

They said they at first thought it was wolves, but when they looked up, they could see two dark animals way up on the steep wall, a place wolves could never go, plus the things were too big for wolves. The howling deteriorated into shrieking, and the things started throwing rocks down the cliffs. Since these things obviously had hands, the kids weren't sure what to think, so they took off, terrified.

Well, Al and I, both in our late 40s, were old geezers compared to these kids, who looked to be in their late teens, if that, and our first thought was that they were playing a trick on us. I mean, the whole story was preposterous, even though they were pretty convincing. But their supposed-fear was contagious enough that we both packed up our gear and followed them back down to the campground.

Once back, the kids asked us to take a group photo of them using their cell phones, which we did, and Al also took one with his camera. After everything was over and done, we later studied that photo, trying to figure out from the looks on their faces if they seemed honest or not, and we had to say that they did. They really seemed genuinely scared.

I guess I have to say that this was the beginning of our refusal to acknowledge that there was something strange in Glacier, something we would later meet in an up-close and personal way. By saying these kids were fooling us, we denied the possibility that what they saw was real, a denial that might have saved us from what we later experienced, though who knows?

Would we have gone home if we'd believed them? Probably not, but we might've been more careful about where we went and what we did, being aware that there were strange creatures out and about.

Well, our first week was up, and as we looked through our photos, I will say we were both very pleased with the results—lots of stunning sunrises and sunsets, as well as photos of aspen and larches in their fall colors, great shots of moose, elk, deer, various birds, and even a few black bears, though no grizzlies, but we were pretty sure we'd see a few over on the other side of the park.

For the transition from the west to the east side of the park, we'd planned a special side trip—we'd hike the Highline Trail to the Granite Park Chalet and spend the night, then hike back out over Swiftcurrent Pass, which would take us to the parking lot at our cabin at the Swiftcurrent Motor Lodge in Many Glacier.

We would leave our car at the cabin there at the start of the hike, then ride the shuttle to the top of Logan Pass, which divided the east and west sides and was also where the Highline started.

By hiking to the Granite Park Chalet, we would see some of the interior of the park and yet not have to carry backpacking gear, as the chalet provided sleeping accommodations, as well as food, if you pre-ordered it, though you had to cook it yourself at the chalet kitchen.

Granite Park Chalet is a small Swiss-looking rock building built in 1914 by the Great Northern Railway as part of their agenda to make Glacier more amenable to tourists. The chalet is accessible only by hiking, and it's like a backcountry hostel. The rooms have bunks, and they provide bedding if you pay extra. It was the perfect setup for us, for with all our photography equipment, carrying overnight gear would be a bit much for two middle-aged guys who were more than a bit out of shape.

When we got off the shuttle at the top of Logan Pass and headed for the Highline, we were at first pretty disappointed, for we weren't expecting to encounter so many people there. The rest of the park was pretty empty because it was so late in the season, but I think every person who visits Glacier has to go see the Highline.

But it didn't take long for the trail to clear out, for after about a third of a mile, you reach a narrow section that turns most people around. I mean, it's maybe four feet wide along a wall with a drop-off of several hundred feet.

If you have a fear of heights, you're not going one step farther, even though the park has installed cables along the wall to hold onto. This section only lasts three-tenths of a mile, but that's an eternity if you're terrified. It did make for some good photos, as well as help clear the crowds.

After that stretch, you hike several miles, then cross Haystack Pass, which is a few hundred feet up a couple of switchbacks, then everything else is pretty much downhill to the chalet. It's a little over six miles, and you're in the heart of Glacier with fantastic views all around, looking across a huge glacial valley to the Livingston Range, which is very picturesque.

Well, we'd stopped for awhile after crossing Haystack Pass and let time get away from us, and having to film a stunning sunset didn't help things, but we weren't too worried, as we knew the chalet wasn't far, maybe a couple of miles. We could easily hike that before dark. We also had our headlamps, so we pretty much just moseyed along.

As it got along toward dusk, I guess it finally dawned on us where we were and that it might be prudent to get a move on. Glacier is famous for its bears, and one doesn't really want to be lollygagging along a trail there in the dark. And just as we upped our pace, we could hear someone coming. It was getting hard to make out much, but we finally saw a man hiking up the trail.

As he got closer, I could see he looked tired, and I wondered why he was hiking out so late, as there was no way he'd make the trailhead at Logan Pass before it was pitch dark. Most of the trail was fairly easy, but the switchbacks over Haystack Pass might be tricky, as well as the wall by the cables.

He looked startled when he saw us, then stopped, saying out of the blue, "Something's following me."

I thought his face looked very white, though it was hard to tell in the twilight.

"Are you camping?" I asked. "Where's your gear?"

He answered, "I was going to the chalet, but I decided to turn around when I heard something growling."

"Growling?" Al asked. "Like a bear? Or wolves? It's really rare for wolves to attack a person, but being out here alone in the dark might not be such a good idea."

The man replied, "I don't normally hike after dark, but I got off work late. I know to make noise to tell bears I'm coming. But if you're going to the chalet, you might want to turn around and hike out with me. I work at the Lake McDonald Lodge, and I've hiked this park for years. I know what wolves sound like, and I can tell you what I heard wasn't wolves—or a bear."

Now Al said, "Well, maybe you should hike to the chalet with us. Whatever was following you, you'll be OK as there's safety in numbers. Bears don't like groups. Better than hiking out alone to Logan."

Al was obviously concerned, trying to talk the guy out of going on by himself. As we stood there, things getting darker by the moment, I could feel the night chill coming on.

"It wasn't a bear," the guy said, shrugging his shoulders. He sat on a nearby rock, catching his breath.

"I'm Jesse," he sighed. "I guess I really should stay with you guys, but the idea of going back seems like the wrong direction. My energy's a bit depleted, and I tend to get a little hypoglycemic."

I dug an apple from my pack and handed it to him, introducing myself and Al. He thanked me, then began munching on it.

"I was about ready to climb a tree," he now said matter-of-factly.

"A tree? Why would you climb a tree?" I asked.

"It felt safer."

As Al and I stood there, waiting for Jesse to eat his apple and get his blood-sugar level back to normal, the most horrible sound I've ever heard before or since came from far below us in the valley. It's hard to describe, but others have said it sounds like a woman screaming, being killed in a most horrible way.

Jesse jumped up, and the three of us stood there in the near dark as Al said, "That was a mountain lion. I've heard them before down in Wyoming. It's a very intimidating sound. The one I heard had just brought down a deer, which I knew because I came across it on my hike out. If you get on the Internet, you might be able to find a recording of one."

"Are you sure that's what it was?" Jesse asked doubtfully.

"No question about it. I'd stake my life that's what was following you. It found a deer for dinner instead. Let's go on to the chalet. We won't have any trouble now."

I don't know why, but I was now feeling a sense of dread. Was I feeding off Jesse's fears? It didn't seem like it, as he seemed pretty calm at that point.

I hesitated, then said, "Al, I think we should listen to Jesse and hike back out. Something's wrong. I can't explain it, but my gut says to turn back."

"It's the lion," Al replied impatiently. "Your gut's telling you a large dangerous predator is near, and it is, but it won't be interested in us anymore. We're not that far from the chalet."

Now, let me say that, having grown up in Pinedale, Wyoming, in the shadow of the mighty Wind River Range, home to grizzlies, and then living in Jackson, near Yellowstone, I've seen and been around my share of large predators, mostly bears. I knew to be cautious, but I wasn't typically afraid like I was that evening out on the trail.

I added, "Al, you know me. I'm not normally afraid, but my intuition says we should go back."

The conversation went back and forth for awhile, Al finally convincing me that I was just feeling the effect of the lion's murderous-sounding yowl. I recalled what the kids up at Avalanche Lake had claimed to have heard and seen, but decided not to bring it up, as I didn't want to scare Jesse even more.

Finally, Al convinced us to head on to the chalet, partly because we knew it was way closer than Logan Pass, and the thought of hiking down the switchbacks at Haystack Pass in the dark was intimidating. We picked up our packs and all headed down the trail, though I noticed Jesse strategically placed himself between Al and me.

We continued on towards the chalet, the shadows lengthening, hiking in silence. Somehow, it seemed that the farther we went, the stranger things felt. It had kind of started with Jesse's comment about climbing a tree—an action that seemed logical but actually wasn't, as most predators can also climb—something someone would think of doing when they weren't thinking rationally.

It got worse and worse until it became a bizarre out-of-focus feeling. It reminded me later of when you get out of a long bout of dental work—you're disoriented and unsure of yourself, and it takes awhile to get back to reality.

Except our reality just kept getting more unreal. I don't think it had anything to do with Jesse personally, but I do think in retrospect he brought it with him, though not intentionally. I think that whatever had been following him was now following us, in spite of Al being so certain it was a big cat that was now sidetracked, feeding on a deer. Al was wrong, as we found out, and wrong in a bad way—a really bad way that he would soon take the brunt of.

We'd never hiked the Highline before, but Jesse had, and he said we were close to the chalet, but it never appeared. We just kept hiking on and on until it was dark enough that we needed our headlamps to continue.

As we stopped to dig them out of our packs, Jesse remarked, "We should've been at the chalet by now. Something's wrong."

"Is it easy to miss?" Al asked.

"No, it's very visible from the trail. Even at night, you can see the inside lights. But I think we somehow passed it."

We decided to continue on for awhile, then reconnoiter, hoping we'd just misjudged the distance, but we soon came to a fork in the trail, a branch leading off to our right. Even though it was fairly dark, we could see the outline of a ridge where it looked like the trail began climbing.

"This is the fork to Swiftcurrent Pass," Jesse said. "We missed the chalet, but it's not far behind us. How we overlooked the cutoff from the main trail is beyond me, but at least now I know where we are."

We turned around, relieved, now following Jesse, but it was only a moment later that we almost ran into him, for he'd stopped smack in the middle of the trail.

"There's something ahead," he said under his breath.

I could tell he was scared, but at least he didn't try to get in between Al and me. We stood there, listening, when suddenly, far in the distance ahead came a mournful howling sound.

Al whispered, "Wolves."

Jesse said simply, "Not wolves."

"Then what is it?" I asked.

"I don't know," Jesse replied, barely audible. "I've heard lots of wolves, and it's not wolves."

I again flashed back on the kids at Avalanche Lake. They'd heard strange howls, then seen the two black figures climbing the wall. I felt a chill go up my spine.

"Let me lead," I said to Jesse. "We have to get to the chalet. Whatever it is, there's three of us and hopefully only one of them."

I nodded to Al as I got out my bear spray, and I noted he did the same. Seeing us, Jesse pointed to his belt, where his spray was already handy, which made sense, since he'd been on high alert before even meeting up with us.

"How far back is the chalet?" I asked Jesse.

"Not far. Watch for a trail that takes off to the right," he replied.

I took my headlamp off my forehead, holding it in my hand so I could more easily scan the trail ahead. I saw nothing unusual, watching carefully for the side trail. We didn't want to miss it again, as it was now almost pitch black.

Fortunately, it wasn't long before it came into view. But as I turned, I caught a glimpse of something off to my left, then saw a large rock coming my way, barely missing me. It was hard to tell, but it looked to be the size of a grapefruit.

I yelled something, though I can't remember what, and it's probably not repeatable anyway, then I ducked as that was followed by another smaller rock that hit my shoulder, making it sting. Now Al was also yelling, and the rocks suddenly started coming in like hail. Whatever was throwing them was strong, as the rocks were big.

Al began picking up the incoming rocks and throwing the ones he could lift back at the shadows, but when Jesse yelled for us to run, we did, following his headlamp up the trail, rocks lobbing in behind us. I had no idea how far the chalet was, but it had to be close or we were goners, for there was no way to even use our bear spray. Whatever or whoever was throwing the rocks was staying hidden in the trees. I again thought of the kids at Avalanche Lake. Hadn't they said the black creatures were throwing rocks?

Everything seemed to slow down, as if it were just a dream. I felt several more large rocks hit my pack, and later, I found one of my lenses had been totally shattered. Al also later found some of his equipment damaged, and we both shuddered to think of what our backs would've looked like if we hadn't been carrying packs.

I could now see dim lights ahead, and I knew it was the chalet. Jesse must've been in much better shape than we were, for he'd completely disappeared. I knew Al was close behind me, as I heard him say, "Dave, don't leave me!"

When I heard him make a loud moan, I knew something was wrong. I stopped and turned, shining my headlamp back, and I could see he was on the ground. Even though I wanted to keep running, I stopped and went to his side.

I knew he'd been hit by a rock. He was trying to get back up, blood streaming down his face, and I reached out to help him, when I saw a hand grab him by the leg. Either the thing's body was out of range of my light or I've repressed what it looked like, but I'll never forget that hand.

I know it was attached to an arm, but it seemed like an entity all on its own, just this big hand with a dark leathery palm and black hair on its back. Its nails were long and thick and a yellow-brown color, as if it had been digging in the dirt. And it was huge, probably three times the size of my hands, and I'm pretty much an average-sized guy at six-feet, not at all small.

As it turned out later after cleaning up Al's head wound, we found that it was just a surface wound with lots of blood, but his real injury was from that hand. It tore up his pants and left several deep marks in his leg that he later had stitched up, but even at that, he now has long scars. He used to wear shorts a lot, but he never does now, as the scars make him look like he was attacked by a vampire.

I was pulling on Al in one direction, and that hand was pulling on his leg, while poor Al was moaning and trying to get up. I felt I was losing the battle, and as I glanced up to see several other dark shadows coming in, I knew I had to do something, and fast. I was no match for even one of these things, yet alone several. And of course, Jesse was long gone.

I held up my bear spray to take off the safety, and the minute I did, the hand let Al go. I knew the creature had to know what bear spray was to react like that. People have said it was a bear, but bears don't have hands like that.

I quickly grabbed Al and pulled him up, his pack falling from his back as I did so. Now, you can tell Al's a true photographer by what he did next, and I find it hard to believe, but he grabbed his pack and pulled his camera from it and began shooting photos. A lot of the more expensive cameras don't have built-in flashes, but Al grabbed his little snapshot camera, which did.

He managed to shoot off a dozen or more photos as I stood there, dumbfounded and unable to move. I'll save you the suspense by saying these creatures vanished so quickly that only a couple of his photos captured anything of interest, and that was just some large shadowy figures with no detail. I know he would've found fame and fortune if they'd turned out.

Suddenly, whereas I'd felt as if I was walking around in a cloud, my head was clear as a bell, and I got Al turned around and headed towards the chalet. Jesse helped us through the door, then we somehow found a chair and examined Al's wounds.

A guy who'd been standing on the upper deck of the stone building was aware something strange had just come down, and he asked if we were OK. Come to find out, he was one of the chalet's caretakers, and after we got Al fixed up as best we could, this guy checked us in and, even though we were late enough that the kitchen was closed, he went in and cooked our pre-ordered dinner for us.

His name was Kevin, and he was a super guy. Al didn't feel much like eating, so Kevin brought him some broth, then we pretty much put Al to bed with some pain-killers that Kevin kept for emergencies. Al had acted like nothing much was going on through the whole thing, and we thought the wound on his head was the extent of it, and it wasn't until the next day we found the deep scratches in his legs, his pants soaked with blood.

I felt really bad about not noticing that sooner but kind of wrote it off to the weird mind space we'd all been in that night. Fortunately, the pack horses had come in that morning from Packer's Roost, bringing in supplies for the chalet, and Al managed to hitch a ride down that way while I walked out with them. The packer guys then gave us a ride to the park headquarters in West Glacier, where a ranger took us to an urgent-care clinic, where they cleaned Al's wounds and stitched them up, then gave him a tetanus shot.

I later got a ride in the park shuttle over to Many Glacier to retrieve our car, thinking our second week's reservations there would be a wash, but after I went and got Al from the clinic, we decided to go on back to the cabin we'd rented and just hang out while he recovered. He would need to return to the clinic several times to have the bandages changed and the wounds cleaned. And though he initially had some pain from the gouges, they healed pretty fast, and his head wound was actually pretty minor, so no problems there.

We spent a pretty quiet week at Many Glacier, and I actually ended up enjoying it. Al wasn't able to walk far, but we got some nice photos from the shores of nearby Swiftcurrent Lake and also took some nice drives to places like St. Mary Lake and Two Medicine. We stuck near the car, but that was OK, as I had no intention of going into the backcountry again, at least not in Glacier.

But what was really interesting was the talk I had with Kevin up at the chalet after Al had gone to bed and Jesse was in his room. Kevin said he'd worked at the chalet for several years, but this would be his last season. When I told him what had happened, he called the creatures Bigfoot and said they were getting bolder and bolder as time went on. We were the first he'd known who had actually been attacked, but he'd heard plenty of stories where hikers had been intimidated and stalked.

Kevin's theory was that these animals were fed up with people, just like me and Al had been with the wedding business, and they were getting more aggressive. He worried about someone eventually being killed, and wondered if some of those who'd gone missing in the park weren't the victims of angry creatures who felt like their territory was being invaded.

This was just his theory, but it makes sense to me, and I can say I pretty much identify with them. It seems like we humans are invading every place more and more, and what's worse is how we act like we're entitled to do so. It's actually pretty sad to me, even though these things almost killed Al, but maybe I'd feel the same way if I were in their shoes.

Both Al and I left the wedding business and went on to other things, tired of the stress and difficult people. He and his wife moved to Casper, Wyoming, where he works at a car dealership, and I stayed in Jackson, doing the night stocking at a grocery store.

I'll retire soon, and when I do, my wife and I are moving back to Pinedale, where I hope to spend most of my time fishing, but not in any places where Bigfoot could potentially hang out, though I know they can pretty much go wherever they please.

And hopefully, if I am in their territory, they'll just make some noise instead of throwing rocks. That's all I'll need to know to move on, just a little growl or two.

9

A GIFT

I've heard a lot of stories about Bigfoot being dangerous, and I know there's some truth to this. However, I've also heard stories like the following, where the opposite seems to be the case.

I met this fellow I'll call Brent in Montana, where he'd come from North Dakota to enjoy the great trout fishing on the Madison River. He told us this story over a Dutch-oven dinner of trout and baked potatoes, with peach cobbler for dessert.

His tale seems to show how your luck can turn one way and then another within hours, and sometimes you're not even aware it's changed—and it also shows how wrong we can sometimes be, though I'll say I can certainly understand his misjudgment. —Rusty

My story happened many years ago, way before Glacier National Park was so popular—you could say back in the good old days before it was discovered, a good 20 years ago.

I have no idea if these beings or Bigfoot or whatever they were are even still in that country. Given all the people that've come in since then, it wouldn't surprise me if they hadn't hightailed it to Canada and points north. I know I would.

In fact, I did, though I hightailed it more to the northeast, over to North Dakota, where I've lived for the past 15 years. It's harsh there in the winter, but I don't have to deal with a lot of people around.

Anyway, that's beside the point, which is mostly that if this had happened today, I would've immediately gotten a ride and never would've seen what I did. But back then, there just wasn't anyone around to give one rides.

So, as you can guess, my vehicle broke down in Glacier National Park. I was just a kid, all of 20, still wet behind the ears, as they say, and I'd managed to buy an old Dodge pickup for a few hundred dollars, which was a fortune back then, at least to me. I'd talked the guy down a few bucks, seeing how the dang thing was all rusted out, but as long as it ran, that's all I cared about.

I'd just gotten myself a job a couple of months before over in East Glacier, working as a grunt for the railroad, helping unload and load luggage and all that for the people who came to visit the park by train. There's a big hotel there, I can't recall its name, but it's a big deal for tourists, very historic, built by the railroad in the 1920s.

Wait, I remember now, it was the Glacier Park Hotel, now called the Glacier Park Lodge. It was quite the deal back when it was built, with teepees and Blackfeet Indians around the grounds, all paid to create this Western experience for the dudes. Of course, by the time I came around, it was just another big old historic hotel that needed some updating, but it still attracted the tourists.

I was living in Kalispell with my folks and younger sister, riding the shuttle bus to East Glacier on Sundays and staying there all week in a free room they gave as part of my pay, though I guess that meant it wasn't actually free. I'd go back home Friday evenings for the weekend.

I'd get homesick, see, which isn't what you're supposed to admit to when you're 20 and supposedly all grown up, so I'd tell my friends I had a gal back there I was going to see. The truth was, I missed my mom and her good homestyle cooking and my dad and his grousing at me and my sis always teasing me...well, you get the picture.

So, it was a big deal the day I'd saved enough to buy my own vehicle. I could now come and go as I pleased, no more waiting around for a bus that was always late. I had wheels, and that meant freedom.

Until the dang truck broke down, that is. And of course it couldn't have happened at a worse place—Logan Pass, at the top of the Going to the Sun Road, or the Sun Road, as we locals called it. Actually, thinking about it, it could've happened along the road where there's no guardrail, or at any number of places that would've been worse, so I guess I was lucky it happened at the top of the pass, where there's a visitor center and big parking lot.

It was, of course, late at night, since these things usually happen at the worst possible time. I'd had to cover for my friend Matt who'd managed to get himself in trouble for being a little too obnoxious the previous evening. He'd actually thrown a chair through one of the hotel windows when some guy asked him to shine his boots or something. Matt really didn't belong in the service industry, as they call it now, as he had a problem with being told what to do, but that's another story.

So, I'd covered for Matt, doing my job and then his, and it was probably around 11 in the evening when I topped over Logan Pass and promptly broke down, my alternator going out. I could tell it was going from the battery gauge, but I was hoping I could at least make it to where I could coast down the west side of the pass.

Nope, no go—so near and yet so far. I was on the edge of the parking lot, but there was no way I could push that thing over to where it would start rolling, so I finally had to abandon ship and start walking. I think I used up every cuss word a 20-year-old knows and then some.

Now days, you could undoubtedly hitch a ride even at that late hour, but back then, things went pretty much dead an hour or so after dark when everyone who'd been on the east side of the park made it back to the west side and vice versa. The park was abandoned by 10, and you had it all to yourself, nary even a ranger, if you were dumb enough to be stuck out there.

Or at least I thought the park was abandoned. I found out otherwise.

OK, so there I was, sitting all alone in my broken-down old truck at the top of Logan Pass at almost midnight. I sat there for awhile, reconnoitering, trying to figure out what to do, though I didn't have many choices.

Actually, I had only two choices. One, I could spend the night in my truck, uncomfortable, but fairly safe, and someone would come by the next day to help me out. For most people, that would be the logical choice.

The other choice was to start walking, heading for civilization, which would be the Lake McDonald Lodge, which I figured was about 10 miles away. There was a very minor chance that I would meet someone who would give me a ride, but it was unlikely.

So, being 20 years old and not very logical, I decided to start walking. It was all downhill, paved, I had a flashlight, and I could make a good three or four miles an hour and probably be down there in a few hours at the most. I had plenty of energy, was in great shape, and shoot, I could even jog along and save myself some time.

It was a beautiful starry night with a half moon, with enough light that I actually wouldn't even need a flashlight. It would be easy to follow the paved highway.

I gathered my small pack, got out and stood there for awhile, letting my eyes get acclimated to the dark, then headed down the road. It was actually starting to feel kind of like an adventure.

Well, it was an adventure, but not anything like I would've predicted, and it was an adventure I'd just as soon forget. And I later found out my estimated 10 miles to the Lake McDonald Lodge was actually more like 20. When you're riding a bus, I guess you don't really pay attention, because I'd been on that road dozens of times.

But I ended up not having to hike it after all, because I got myself into—how should I put it—a sticky situation.

Now, before I go on, I should mention something you've probably already guessed—I was pretty cocky back in my youth, though this incident kind of knocked the wind out of me some. I would just jump to conclusions sometimes, though this particular night brought a little humility into my life, which was a good thing.

Well, when I started down the road, it was at first kind of spooky, being all alone out there. The Sun Road is carved out of the side of a huge spine called the Garden Wall, and it's narrow with hairpin turns and drops off the side thousands of feet. Some of the west side has a rock wall for a guardrail, but it's low enough that one could easily stumble right over it, so I tried to keep to the inside wall as much as possible.

It took awhile, but my eyes gradually adjusted to the dark to the point I could make out the stripe down the center of the road, which was a big help. Like I said, it was spooky walking along, sensing those immense depths just right beside you, hoping to not accidentally walk right off the edge.

After awhile, I'd kind of gotten a rhythm going, and it wasn't too long before I could tell I'd come to what's called Big Bend, which is a turnout where cars can pull off and stop to enjoy the views, though it was more often where people stopped to regain their nerve from driving the scary road.

I knew I'd gone about two miles at that point, and I paused to look at the night sky, where more stars than I thought could ever exist all hung right there in front of me, shining like an iridescent magic carpet. It was impressive, and I suddenly felt very lucky to be there, the only human on that mountain, as far as I knew. I was almost glad my truck had broken down, otherwise I would've probably never seen such an amazing sight.

Looking back, I think this overwhelming feeling of awe was the reason I ignored another feeling that was seeping into my conscious-ness—one of trepidation and maybe even fear. If I hadn't ignored it, I think I would've at that point just walked right back up to my truck and spent the night there.

Well, it is what it is, and I started back down the road, picking up my pace a little, feeling a little tenuous and ignoring the fact I was getting scared. I'd probably walked another quarter-mile when I got the feeling that something was following me.

Now, Logan Pass is famous for its mountain goats, sheep, and other critters, many which are habituated to humans and unafraid, so I just figured it was something like a mountain goat checking me out and following along. I can't say I liked the idea, but it didn't seem particularly troublesome.

I stopped several times and turned around, hoping to see whatever it was, but it seemed like it somehow intuited my actions and would also stop. Had I actually heard anything? I wasn't sure, but if I had, it would be the sound of hooves, which meant it was a sheep or goat, yet I hadn't heard a thing.

I decided it was time for my headlamp, as much as I didn't want to use it. I'd read that it takes a good half-hour for your night vision to kick in, and using my headlamp would put me back to ground zero. But it occurred to me that it could be a bear, and I would therefore probably be wise to figure out what was going on. A bear's paws wouldn't make any noise, which would account for me thinking there was something following yet hearing nothing.

I'd put my headlamp on when leaving the truck, so all I had to do was reach up and turn it on. It had a red-light setting that was made specifically to preserve one's night vision, so I clicked it to that and quickly turned around.

There was nothing there. I turned the light back off and listened for the longest time, but heard nothing. I decided I was just being paranoid, so once again continued back down the road.

The thought of being followed by a bear wasn't a pleasant one, for most bears give humans a wide berth. Very few bears are predatory, so I hoped that maybe it was just curious, assuming that's what it was.

I was now wanting to just get down to where there were other people around, away from what was becoming a feeling of vulnerability. I still refused to admit I was scared, though something didn't feel right. Being afraid wasn't part of my makeup, and the few times I had been scared, I'd quickly tucked it in and gotten over it.

Now, all of a sudden, seemingly from nowhere, I thought I heard someone say something, someone behind me. This made me think, I can tell you, for it hadn't even occurred to me that maybe another person was following me.

If so, why? Were they wanting to rob me? It didn't make sense. You don't pick random strangers walking down a remote highway in the middle of the night to rob. Well, maybe you do, but you don't follow them on foot. And who would be out in the middle of Glacier at night? I hadn't seen another vehicle at the pass.

Anyway, at that point nothing made much sense, it was all so vague. I had a sixth sense that I was being followed, yet I couldn't hear or see anything, except for one slight noise that sounded maybe like someone talking, which was probably just a nighthawk. I was beginning to think I was getting paranoid, though I'd never been afraid of being alone in the dark before.

But I just couldn't shake that creepy feeling. In fact, it was getting stronger the farther I walked. I stopped and again shone my light all around, but saw nothing.

I could now hear the sound of running water, and I knew I was approaching the Weeping Wall, a place where water cascades down onto the road. Sometimes it's just a few trickles, and other times, it's like a curtain of water. I'm not sure if it's coming down from some drainage above or if it's seeping from the wall itself, but as I got closer, I realized the wall was going great guns. The water was spraying clear into the middle of the road.

As I approached it, my hair began standing on end, and I don't mean that figuratively. It was literally standing on end, just as if I'd stuck my finger in a socket. I had a friend tell me once about climbing and almost getting hit by lightning, and he described his hair doing that exact same thing right before lightning struck only a short distance away, literally knocking him off his feet.

I have no idea why I reacted like I did, but I quickly slipped through the water and up against the Weeping Wall. Did I somehow think water would be a good thing to deflect an electrical charge? No, I knew better than that. If anything, it would increase the shock. I don't know what I was thinking, but in retrospect, I think I simply wanted to hide.

But I didn't get shocked, and the charge seemed to go away. I stood there, wondering why I'd decided to get wet like that, ice-cold water dripping off me, thinking that my truck was now about three miles up the road, way too far to make a run for, and wondering why my hair would stand on end like that.

I now saw something coming along the road in the moonlight. It looked to be wearing a dark cloak, for its head and shoulders seemed to flow together with no definable neck. It was tall, maybe a good seven feet, and like its neck, its arms seemed to flow into its body. I'm not describing this very well, but it looked like its arms were concealed by some sort of cloak it was wearing.

The creepy feeling was really strong now, so much so that I wanted to run, and it was all I could do to stand still and be quiet. It was right by me, not more than 20 feet away, when it paused. I was sure it had spotted me, but it continued on.

I was now shaking, and it wasn't all from standing under a sheet of ice water. I wondered what I'd just seen—it didn't seem human, and yet, what else could it be? I waited, wondering if it was alone or if more like it would eventually come along.

I had no idea what to do next. I couldn't just stay there hiding in the water, as I would freeze to death. If I went back to my pickup, what was there to keep this thing from following? And even if I made it back to the truck, I had no defense except hiding inside it, and this creature looked like it could easily break a window or two. Should I continue on down the road, following it, hoping it wouldn't turn around and see me?

I felt stuck.

I then began assessing my other possible options. I could attack it, coming up behind and using the element of surprise, crowning it with a big rock. I mean, it looked big and scary, but I hadn't even seen its face. Maybe it was old and not as strong as it looked.

Or maybe I could cross over the low rock wall along the highway and hide, then wait for daylight. I did have a light, and I could use it to scope out how steep it was.

I tried to recall the terrain around the Weeping Wall, and all I could remember was that it was the side of the mountain, like the rest of the Going to the Sun Road, and went straight off. I knew my odds of finding a place to hide were pretty slim.

How about climbing the wall on the inside? Same thing. Sheer cliffs and hopeless.

I waited, getting colder by the minute. I knew I had to do something.

Now, like I said, I could be kind of cocky, and for some reason, that cockiness kicked in. I stood there, getting colder and colder and madder and madder. I had done nothing to this person or thing, so why were they following me, scaring me to where I couldn't think straight?

I stepped out from the water, wondering if I could ever warm up again, now soaking wet. Thinking about this made me even madder. I'd been minding my own business, trying to walk down to get help, and this creature thing had messed everything up.

I was now no longer afraid, and I knew I had to start moving or I'd start shivering again. So, without even thinking about it, I started jogging down the highway, once again heading for the Lake McDonald Lodge. If I caught up with the thing in black, well, so be it. Maybe I had a few choice words for it for scaring me so badly.

It didn't take long to get a hitch in my side, and I had to stop, breathing heavily. After resting for a moment, I decided that I needed to get a more reasonable pace going, slow down a little and find a speed I could sustain.

I started out again, this time much slower, just a slow jog, a pace I could probably manage for some time. It would warm me up, and I immediately began to feel better, like I had some control over things.

That was, until I came around a corner and felt that strange charge again. This time, my hair didn't stand on end because it was wet, but I could feel it, like I'd run into an electrical field of some kind. It's hard to describe, but if you've ever gotten a mild shock and felt a little disoriented afterwards, well, it was like that, a sense of uneasiness and disorientation.

I could now see something dark against the inside wall along the highway. I paused, trying to make it out better. Was it the thing I'd seen earlier, or was it just a dark spot along the highway, maybe some vegetation growing along the wall?

As I got nearer to it, I could tell it wasn't vegetation, for it stepped out onto the road, as if it was going to try and stop me. Like I said before, I didn't like the way it made me feel—I guess scared would be the best way to describe it.

Was this thing out to get me? I had no idea. It hadn't shown any such tendency, but I'd figured that was because it hadn't seen me standing there behind the wall of water. Because it was big and dark and mysterious, I just assumed the worst. And now, as I put on a burst of speed to run around it, I knew without doubt it was going to try to grab me as I went by.

And as this huge shadow stepped directly towards me, I let out a bellow that would raise the dead. I went running by, yelling at the top of my lungs, and it stopped and watched as I ran by like a banshee. In retrospect, it made no attempt to catch me or anything, it just stood and watched me go by.

I was soon past it, unhindered, and then ran right smack into the low retaining wall along the outside of the highway. I almost caught myself, but then managed to go right over and down the side of the cliff. I'd been so focused on the shadow that I'd failed to notice that the highway curved.

They say time slows down when something like that happens, but if anything, it sped up. I was over that rock wall before I even knew what was happening, falling through space, anticipating the oncoming harsh end to my short life.

A few seconds later, I landed with a crunch on what must've been a small ledge or even a large rock sticking out of the mountainside. I hung there above what felt like thousands of feet of empty air. I could see a bush growing nearby, so I grabbed onto that, the wind knocked out of me, amazed that I'd landed where I did. After catching my breath, I realized I was uninjured, which was a miracle.

I later went back and tried to find the exact spot where I'd landed, and I found a small ledge jutting out of the cliff, several bushes growing out of it, which had caught me and broken my fall. Talk about luck!

The entire sequence of events seemed not just improbable, but impossible. Just a couple of hours before, I'd been merrily driving my pickup across the pass, and now here I was on a ledge, hanging onto a bush for dear life, afraid to move. How could things change so drastically and so quickly? And if you've ever watched someone do something totally insane, like walk a tight rope across a gorge with no safety line, you'll know what I mean when I say my heart was in my mouth with apprehension.

I could now see something dark looking over the edge, and I knew it was the cloaked thing. I again felt the electrical charge, and I watched in horror as it looked like it was assessing the climb down to me, both of its legs now hanging over the rock wall.

I began yelling, "No, don't do it, you'll fall," and other inane things, afraid it would come after me and knock me off my perch. I could now tell that I was only maybe 15 feet down, and it dawned on me that if I'd fallen any farther, I would've been going too fast for anything to save me. But that fifteen feet might as well have been a hundred or more, for climbing back up was impossible.

I now heard a couple of deep thuds on the road above me, and it occurred to me that the creature was collecting rocks to throw to knock me off. I can't begin to tell you the sense of dread I felt, and I actually began crying.

It again looked over at me, and I waited for it to throw down rocks, but it just stood there, watching me for what seemed like forever, not moving.

It suddenly hit me how fatigued I was, which I later realized was primarily from the stress. I wanted badly to sleep, but I knew if I did, I'd fall. I stubbornly held on through what was probably the longest night of my life.

At some point, the creature left, and I gradually began to see the faint light of dawn. I couldn't believe that I'd made it through the night, and I felt a sense of elation that since it was now daylight, I would soon be rescued.

But that elation quickly turned to despair when it dawned on me that no one could see me down there, and there was no reason for anyone to stop and look over the edge. Not only that, knowing the Going to the Sun Road, there wasn't any place to stop even if someone wanted to. I could potentially hang there all day and no one would know the difference, though I knew I actually couldn't hang there much longer.

I now thought I heard the sound of a car coming in the distance. It was barely daylight, but I knew that tourists came out early to watch the sunrise and get a good parking spot on Logan Pass, as there are lots of hiking trails there.

I could hear it coming closer, and I wondered if it would hear me yelling as it went by, though it seemed doubtful. I waited, wanting to time my yelling just right. But to my disbelief, the car sounded like it stopped right above me. I could then hear a car door close as if someone had gotten out.

I yelled and yelled as loud as I could, thinking maybe I was just imagining things and there was no one there at all, until I saw someone look over the edge down at me.

A voice now said, "What are you doing down there? Are you OK?"

I couldn't tell for sure, but I somehow knew it was a park ranger, probably coming to check everything out first thing in the morning. I was unable to say anything and just hung there, feeling weaker and weaker.

I could hear the crackle of a radio and I knew the ranger was calling for help. He was soon back over at the edge, telling me to hang on, that help was coming.

It was probably another 20 minutes before I heard a siren and other vehicles coming, and I was soon being hitched into a harness and hauled up to the road by two other rangers who had roped down to where I was.

It seemed impossible, but I was saved. They put me in an ambulance and wanted to take me to the hospital for an assessment, but I didn't want to go, so they took me to the park headquarters instead. After drinking some hot coffee and eating a couple of candy bars, I could feel my strength returning.

My dad came and got me and took me home, and he then hired a tow truck to retrieve my pickup from the top of the pass. A couple of days later, he and I replaced the alternator, and I went back to work.

On my way back to East Glacier, I decided to stop at the park headquarters to thank them, plus I needed the answer to a question I had. When they asked what exactly had happened, I simply said I'd been walking in the dark and went off the edge, which was pretty much the truth, though I didn't tell them about the black creature.

The thing I wanted to know was why the ranger had stopped where I was, as if he knew I was there. He told me he hadn't known I was there at all, but had no choice but to stop, because several large rocks had fallen onto the highway, blocking it. It was just luck, he said.

As I drove my old pickup back up to the top of Logan Pass, I thought about what he'd said. I knew it wasn't just luck, that it was instead the helping hand of someone that I had badly misjudged, a dark creature in the night who hadn't meant me any harm at all, and who had instead helped rescue me, all while unintentionally giving me a gift—the gift of humility.

10

THE ADOPTED NEPHEW

I met Bob when my wife and I decided to visit Glacier and take one of the famous Red Bus tours. He was our driver and one of the better tour guides we'd had. On our way back, when we were almost to the Lake McDonald Lodge where we'd started, he slowed way down for a moment, then continued on.

When someone asked why, thinking maybe he'd spotted a bear or something, Bob just said something about checking for his adopted nephew. It didn't make much sense, so later, once we got back, I asked him about it. Here's the unusual story he told. —Rusty

Rusty, as you know, I'm a driver, also known as a jammer, for the Red Bus Company in Glacier. We're called jammers because the early buses were hard to drive and one had to jam the gears into place, so the early drivers were called gearjammers, which eventually was shortened to jammers.

We're talking back in the 1930s, when the first buses were put into service hauling tourists around the park. The Red Buses are a long tradition, and you'll still see some of the early buses being used. There's no mistaking their long red bodies with the canvas tops one can open when the weather's good, turning them into convertibles. Lots of folks have toured Glacier from the seats of these fine vehicles.

My job is, of course, seasonal, which is partly why I like it. After the busy tourist season, I head south to Arizona, where I hang out in a little casita I own in the town of Ajo, which is close to the border and never gets snow. In a way, I have the best of both worlds—the stunning landscape of Glacier in the summer and the quiet warm Mohave desert in the winter.

There's more to the job than just driving people around—jammers are also tour guides, which means they need to know a lot about the park in order to answer questions and entertain people. And they're also mediators, for it never fails that some people want the top open and some don't, and it can end up in heated arguments. I've actually had to threaten to turn the bus around and go back if people didn't stop arguing, and there have even been a few times that I've done just that.

Well, I usually pick people up at Apgar over on the west side, then drive to Logan Pass and sometimes on to St. Mary. I thought I knew a lot about the park, for I'd worked in and out of Glacier for a number of years, right out of high school, but one day, I found out I didn't know as much as I thought. I knew all about elk and deer and bears and marmots and all the more common mammals, as well as a lot of the birds, but there was one species living here I was totally ignorant of, as are many.

Anyway, I'd been a jammer for at least five years when something strange happened to me. Actually, thinking back, I'd heard a rumor not long after I started about one jammer quitting and leaving the area because he had some kind of a strange encounter. Nobody would really talk about it, so I always assumed it was with a grizzly or something like that, or even with a tourist.

I didn't think much about it, for it's hard to analyze something so vague and catalogue it with things you should worry about, especially since you already have a list that includes accidents, bears, and crazy people.

Anyway, my story began one late evening when I was bringing a bus back to Apgar from Logan Pass. It was cold and rainy, and most of the tourists were hanging out in front of fireplaces.

I'll never forget this guy—the only guy on the tour. He was an older fellow, probably in his late 70s, and he didn't have a shy bone in his body. He was actually quite boisterous, and his voice carried so well I could hear him over the sound of the bus engine even though he was sitting way in the back.

We were coming down the west side of the pass real slow, as the road was wet and it was cold enough I worried about it icing up that late in the day.

This old guy, who I'll call Fred, was going on and on about how some waiter down at the Lake McDonald Lodge had shorted him a few dollars from lunch and how he needed to get back so he could catch him before he left for the day and get his money back.

When I suggested the waiter may have thought it was his tip, Fred got all flustered and accused me of standing up for the guy because we were friends, even though I had no idea who this waiter even was.

This went on and on until it became almost funny in its own way as Fred got more and more worked up. I knew I for sure wouldn't be getting a tip from this guy, so I decided to cut the tour short and get on back.

By then we were at the bottom of the pass, where I would sometimes stop at the Trail of the Cedars and let people get out and stretch their legs and walk around the big trees. But it was raining, and Fred was making me want to be rid of him, so I just passed the turnoff and kept going.

Now, this made Fred even madder. How he knew I sometimes stopped there I'll never know, as it wasn't advertised as part of the tour, but he started in on me and how I was cutting his tour short. At that point, I wanted to stop and leave the guy by the side of the road, but I instead turned around and went back to the parking lot for the trail.

Now, the Trail of the Cedars is a beautiful place, and I always enjoy stopping there, but it does have a few spooky stories associated with it. A number of people have claimed to see this Bigfoot-like thing there, and it certainly does have that feeling, you know, sort of an otherworldly aura when you're standing there looking at those really big old trees, especially when it's rainy and misty. There's a mystique about it.

So, Fred and I got out of the bus and stood there in the rain. I was secretly hoping he'd get cold and want to leave right away, but no, he insisted we go out on the boardwalk to see the trees, even though it now started raining even harder.

Well, he poked around, examining each tree, trying to figure out how big its circumference was, and by then, I was hoping he'd get chilled and maybe die from pneumonia, but he just kept on. It was nearly dark, and I finally told him we had to get back, so he reluctantly turned around and slowly started back toward the bus, now complaining again about how I was cutting his tour short, even though by then we'd actually gone an hour over.

I was beginning to think he was pulling my chain, purposely trying to irritate me. Maybe it was his way of entertaining himself, I thought, by abusing people. Now he was examining some big ferns, even though it was pouring, so I decided it was time to pull out the big guns and get this show on the road.

I stepped off the trail behind him, then made a low moaning noise, then started running towards the bus, acting like I was scared to death. Of course, Fred also took off running, jumping in behind me, and I started the engine and took off, all panicky acting.

As I pulled back out onto the highway, Fred asked, "What was that?"

I told him about how the Cedars area had lots of strange tales and how I'd heard something moaning and how we needed to get back ASAP.

Well, Fred looked kind of skeptical, yet half-scared, and he then proceeded to crawl up into the passenger seat next to me. He settled himself in just in time to yell, "Watch out!" as something emerged from the shadows along the road and stepped right smack in front of the bus.

I hit the brakes so hard it made the bus careen, and I thought I was going to lose control, but I managed to stay on the road.

"You just hit a bear!" Fred informed me, as if I had no clue I'd just hit something.

I started slowly backing up to where a dark form lay in the road, rain pouring down on it so hard it was impossible to make out what it was. I felt sick. I'd never hit any kind of animal before in my life.

I pulled the bus over next to it so I could see what it was, as there was no way I was going to get out, especially if it was a bear. It was probably just wounded, as I hadn't been going all that fast when I hit it. And before I could say anything, Fred was out of the bus, walking around to it and leaning over the dark form.

Suddenly, he was running, and I've never seen anyone move so fast! He was back in the bus and yelling for me to go before I could even process what was happening. I instinctively gunned it, thinking the bear was still alive, and drove away in the pouring rain.

Even though it was now dark, I could make out a look of sheer terror on the old guy's face, and I have to admit to feeling like he deserved it. First, he was making my life miserable with his constant criticism, then he'd insisted on poking around in the trees, even though it was raining, and I'd felt he was doing it on purpose, just to make my day longer. Then, against all common sense, he'd jumped out of the bus and gone back to look at a potentially dangerous animal. I felt that he deserved whatever he was feeling.

He sat silent all the way back to Apgar, the first time he'd kept his mouth shut on the entire tour. I admit I was enjoying not just the silence, but the fact that he'd got some sort of comeuppance. It felt like just desserts.

We were soon back, where I parked the bus and let him out, then said, "I'll call the rangers and let them know about the bear."

"It wasn't a bear," Fred said quietly.

I was surprised. "Was it dead? What was it?"

I thought maybe I'd hit a moose or something, as I knew it was big.

"It wasn't anything I've ever seen before," Fred said. He looked like he was crying, but I decided it was rain and not tears. I couldn't picture the old codger crying about anything.

Fred now took hold of my arm and said, "It was definitely dead, and I'm glad for it. Look, young man, you need to quit this job and get the heck out of here. I'm leaving in the morning. You don't want to work here. These things are real, and they'll kill you if they have half a chance. It wasn't a bear."

He then turned and walked into the lodge.

I wasn't sure what to think, but I knew my next step was to call a ranger. He asked me to drive out with him to show him where this thing was, so off we went in the pouring rain. By then, I was wishing I had a job in a grocery store or a machine shop or anyplace indoors.

Well, we got to the spot where I'd hit the bear or whatever it was, but there was nothing there. Not a thing. We both got out and looked around, and I found a small patch that might be blood, but it wasn't anything definitive. I was beginning to think both Fred and the accident were figments of my imagination.

We went on back to Apgar, where I got my car and went home, tired and ready for dinner. And as I went to sleep that night, I thought again of Fred and the look on his face, wondering why he'd been so upset, thinking of how he'd said it wasn't a bear and yet wouldn't say what it was.

Well, I didn't really think much more about it, as life goes on. I was busy driving buses and dealing with tourists and with demanding bosses and all the daily things that get in one's way. But I will say that every time I drove by that spot, I wondered what I'd actually hit, then I'd wonder about Fred and what he'd thought he saw, because by then, I was thinking he'd thought he'd seen something strange and actually hadn't. I'd decided that, based on how crotchety he was and how his mind worked, that he was messing with me to the bitter end.

Now, the spot I hit this thing at was between the Trail of the Cedars parking lot and the Lake McDonald Lodge. This part of the highway is fairly straight and flat, with McDonald Creek on one side and thick forest on the other, then you eventually come to the lakeshore. There are no steep cliffs or anything like that, and the only big rocks I've ever noticed along there are in the creek bed, which is down somewhat lower than the road.

I mention this because one evening, at almost dark, I was driving a Red Bus along there, bringing it back to the west side of the park for service, as it had started acting up, and we'd put the tourists in another bus. As I got exactly to where I'd hit this thing, a huge rock came flying alongside the bus, nearly hitting it, bouncing along the road and back down into the creek. That rock had to have come from the creek itself, and whoever threw it—and it had to have been thrown—was incredibly strong, or else they had some sort of device like a catapult, because that rock was heavy.

It took me a moment to process what had happened. I at first thought I was lucky to have avoided a rockfall, but then I thought about it and realized there was no place there for rockfall to come down. I finally realized the rock had to have been thrown, and it wasn't meant as a joke, as it was large enough to kill me. I went back the next day and found actual divots in the pavement where it had bounced along.

That day, as I stopped there to look, I started feeling scared. It was totally irrational in my mind, but there I stood in broad daylight, cars going past, and I was scared. Scared of what? I don't know, maybe of whatever threw that rock.

I eventually heard about this happening to other Red Bus drivers coming through there in the evening, enough times it was no coincidence. Like me, they all felt the rocks had to have been thrown. One rock hit a fender, and another actually hit the hood, putting a huge dent in it.

Nobody could figure it out, but I knew it had something to do with whatever I'd hit. Was it revenge? I didn't know, but I did know someone was eventually going to get hurt. And of course, I hadn't mentioned hitting something there to anyone but the ranger, so I was the only one who had an inkling of what might be going on.

I got to where I refused to drive through there in the late evening, and to be honest, it was because I feared for my life. But there was more than that—after awhile, when I'd go by that spot, I started feeling a really deep sense of sadness, like I'd been a part of some tragedy, even though it had been an accident.

I felt that I'd unwittingly become a player in some kind of drama that I didn't want to be in and that I didn't even understand. I wished there was some way I could say I was sorry. There was no need for revenge on innocent people.

I finally told my girlfriend about all this, as I needed someone to talk to. She was a very kind person, and I was sure she'd have some suggestions, and sure enough, she did. She told me I needed to quit *feeling* like I was sorry and instead start *acting* like I was sorry.

Well, that seemed cryptic enough. Act like I was sorry. How? Of course, she was gone to work before I could even ask her if she had anything more definitive to add, so I was on my own. I mulled this over all day, then it dawned on me—if this was a bear, why not leave something there that bears liked? Maybe a bushel of apples or something like that?

Then I thought again of Fred. He'd said it wasn't a bear. What else could it be? Well, something that could throw rocks, or so it seemed.

On my day off, I drove down by Flathead Lake to one of the roadside stands and bought a bunch of fruit—cherries and apples and pears. I also bought a half-dozen pumpkins, some blueberries, and some squash. I spent a fortune, and was feeling pretty silly before I was done. Who was I giving this to again?

That evening, but not too late, I drove back into the park and left a pile of food there by the road where I'd hit this thing, kind of half-hidden so I wouldn't get a ticket if a ranger came by. I'm sure they would've considered it littering—either that or feeding the wildlife, both of which are illegal.

I watched for a minute, then took off, half-scared I'd get a rock lobbed at me. The next morning, when I drove my Red Bus by that spot, I could see it was all gone. So, I did the same thing the next night, then the next and the next until all the fruit and stuff I'd bought was gone.

Something was obviously taking it, as there was never anything left, and each time I'd stop, I'd think back to what Fred had said that whatever it was, it would be happy to kill me. Actually, he'd said, "These things are real, and they'll kill you if they have half a chance." I never spent much time there, I'd just drop the stuff off and get out as fast as I could.

Well, I'd run out of fruit, and I was beginning to think I was nuts, putting out all this expensive food when I didn't even know what was eating it. Sure, there hadn't been any more reports of rock attacks, but that could just be a coincidence.

Whatever was going on, I was tired of spending money and sneaking around so the rangers wouldn't see me. Was I going to have to keep doing this forever as a kind of extortion to keep the other drivers and myself safe?

I decided I needed to know what was going on, to actually see what I was feeding, even though I wasn't sure I wanted to know. So, I headed back down to the roadside stand and bought more fruit and whatnot, but this time, they had some big tubs of local honey, so I bought several of those. Man, this was getting expensive.

That evening, I set out some fruit and one of the tubs, its lid off, then I parked down the road a ways and hiked back with my binoculars. It was almost dark, so I didn't have high hopes of seeing much, but I had to try.

This was an act of courage for me, mind you, for Fred's words kept coming to mind about the thing wanting to kill me. Ironically, I'd killed it, and I suspected it was its friends or family who wanted revenge. At least if they killed me, maybe they'd quit going after the other buses, though I wasn't sure I was altruistic enough to give up my life like that.

I hid behind some bushes and watched. Several cars went by, and it was soon dark. It was getting pretty spooky out there, and there was no way I could see anything, so I finally chickened out and went back to my car, thinking it had been a stupid idea from the git go.

Just as I got in my car, I heard the most forlorn and strange howling. It started out low and then went higher and higher, then back to low again. I swear this went on for a good 20 seconds, and I wondered what kind of animal had lungs like that. And I can say that I had a very strong urge to get out of there.

Well, that howl scared me to death, but what really got to me was that as I drove away, I noticed that my grandfather's necklace was no longer hanging from my rear-view mirror. I guess I should tell you about that necklace so this will make sense.

When I was a kid, my grandpa gave me an arrowhead made of a translucent black glass that he'd found when he'd been a smoke jumper in Wyoming. I put it on a leather neck string and wore it for years, then finally hung it on my rear-view mirror in his memory. It really meant a lot to me, especially when I found out from an archaeologist friend that it was a genuine obsidian Blackfeet arrowhead.

So, when I saw my necklace was missing, it gave me a real jolt. I knew it had been there when I stopped, without a doubt. When I got out, I'd left the window open, and I wasn't gone very long, so whoever took it had done it quickly. I couldn't figure it out, as I was parked on a little side turnout, and my car wasn't even visible from the main highway. In any case, I was bummed out.

The very next day, a fellow Red Bus driver, Andrea, came by where I was waiting near the hotel, wanting to talk to me. She made sure there was no one around, then she said, "Bobby, some of us know what you're doing out there. Word's out about you hitting something and now feeding it. We're all pretty concerned about that."

I was shocked. How did they know? Someone had seen me, or maybe my girlfriend had casually mentioned it to a friend, and you know how those things go. Or had the ranger said something? Did he know I was feeding it?

I started to tell Andrea I was no longer feeding anything, when she added, "I want you to know Gabby saw those things last night on her way in. Trust me, Bobby, you don't want to be feeding them."

Gabby was a fellow bus driver. She'd seen something?

"What did she say it looked like?" I asked.

Andrea replied, "She said it was huge and black and had red eyes. There were two of them, and they were standing right there where we know you've left food. When they saw her, they started running, but one had a bad limp. Trust me, you don't want these things around."

I wasn't sure what to say, so I kind of lamely said I'd stopped feeding them, which was what I was planning on doing anyway.

But all that day, I thought about what Gabby had said—one was limping. Maybe I hadn't killed it after all. That made me feel better, I can tell you, and that evening, I went and got a big tub of sweet corn and took it out there. It was almost dark, but I didn't care. For some reason, I wasn't afraid any more. I even walked all over looking for my grandpa's necklace, but didn't find it.

Even though I'd planned to stop feeding them, hearing that the one was injured and not dead, I kept on putting food out, and I can tell you, it was starting to get expensive. But I wanted to help it out.

Finally, my girlfriend started telling her friends I'd just adopted my teenaged nephew, and he was eating me out of house and home. If anyone had extra garden goods, they should bring them by.

I laughed at this, but before I knew it, I had all kinds of stuff, and even though I started putting more food out, it would all be gone the next day. Andrea and Gabby never said anything, so I don't know if they knew or not, but I didn't care anyway, as long as they didn't tell the rangers.

Finally, along towards late autumn, not long before the park typically shuts down from snowfall, I went to put out more corn, and I saw the stuff I'd left the day before was still there.

I suspected they were gone, probably migrating somewhere else, somewhere warmer and less snowy. But I left that day's food anyway, just in case.

But as I turned to go, that's when I saw it—my grandpa's arrowhead necklace! It had been hung on a tree near the food. Had they taken it while I was trying to watch them with my binoculars? They must have, which means they were very close—and yet, they didn't harm me.

I guess I'd been forgiven. It was ironic, because the one had stepped out in front of the bus, and there was no way I would've intentionally hit it. But maybe they didn't realize that.

The next day, I went back, but all the food was still there. They were definitely gone.

The next spring, as a test, I left some apples in the food spot, but nothing ate them and they were rotting when I picked them back up. There were no more reports of rocks being flung at Red Buses, so I guess they found a new and better place.

But every time I drive by there, I slow down and look, and when people ask why, I just say it's where my adopted nephew used to hang out. I've gotten lots of strange looks, but to date, Rusty, you're the first to actually ask about it.

And so, now you know. I occasionally think of that guy Fred, the one with me when I hit the creature, and I now recognize that he left me with a fear that was probably unfounded.

I will say that if he ever comes back around, I think I'll leave him out there and hope my Bigfoot friends come back and take him home with them.

11

THE MUDPACK

[If you've read my "Montana Bigfoot Campfire Stories," you've read the following story. I'm including it here in case you haven't read it, as it took place in Glacier.]

I met Kelly while fishing on the beautiful Yampa River down near Split Mountain in northwest Colorado near Dinosaur National Monument.

Sarah and I had taken the weekend off and gone to see the famous dinosaur quarry, then I had to give the fishing a shot there on the Yampa at an old family fishing hole that my grandfather once frequented. He wasn't a fly-fisherman, like I am, but would just bait a hook with a worm and toss it into the water, kind of old school, and he always had great success.

I didn't catch one fish, but I did meet Kelly, who was hanging around waiting for his girlfriend to show up. She was on her way back from seeing a herd of wild horses with a friend who lived in nearby Vernal, Utah. As a botanist, Kelly had decided he'd prefer to hang out by the river and take photos of the wildflowers.

I was glad he had, after hearing this story, for I don't think I would've met him otherwise. —Rusty

. . .

R usty, I used to work for Glacier National Park as a seasonal botanist, and I hope you'll mention that Glacier was where this actually happened. Since Glacier is getting to be so popular, people need to know what's out there. There's much more than the infamous grizzly bears you're told to watch out for.

My job that fateful summer was to help do a survey of invasive plants in the park. We always worked together in teams of two, mostly for safety reasons, as bears are less likely to harass groups of people. Even though a pair isn't really a group, the park was trying to accomplish its objectives on a budget, yet they didn't want us out there working alone.

And if my partner in crime hadn't been sick from a case of giardia, I wouldn't have been alone that particular day, and this probably wouldn't have happened, but who's to say? My co-worker's water filter quit working, and he got sick.

This was the second week he'd been out sick, so by then I was used to being alone. I knew I was breaking protocol by going out, but it was that or take the time off, and I needed the money. My supervisor had left it up to me, as I knew the risks.

Well, so I thought I did, which was a fallacy, I found out later. A lot of our work had been at lower elevations, more along streams and rivers, where invasive species would have an easier time getting a hold on things. We would map out what we were finding and also try to eradicate what we could. For larger patches of weeds, a team would come in later and focus on eradication.

But that particular week, I decided to head more into the high country and see how things were doing up at timberline and in the tundra, as we hadn't done much surveying there.

I think, in retrospect, that I was enjoying the solitude and simply wanted a break, as I knew the odds of finding much up there were pretty slim. I was wrong about that, though what I found wasn't necessarily in the realm of botany.

I was backpacking in, and I planned on setting up a base camp, then surveying all around it in concentric circles or grids, depending on the topography, just as we did in the lower areas of the park. But once up in the tundra, all on my own, I started just wandering around, enjoying the stunning beauty of the Northern Rockies. It's a stupendous place—indescribable, really.

Actually, I was almost in Canada, not far from Waterton Lakes National Park. I'd come in that way, as it provided a much easier and closer access to where I wanted to be. I had a tourist boat bring me all the way up the Waterton lakes (there are three, the upper, middle, and lower) and drop me off at Goat Haunt, where I spent my first night in the campground there.

I then hiked along the Waterton River on the Waterton Valley Trail, which is the headwaters for the lakes. Once I got to where Valentine Creek flows into the river, I veered off trail, bushwhacking up the creek and on to where I was under mighty Kootenai Peak. It was stunning country, and I was thoroughly enjoying myself, in spite of the thick alders I had to push through, yet again wondering how I'd managed to get paid to be in such incredible country.

After awhile, I got tired of the bushwhacking and climbed up the slopes of the mountain until I was right at timberline, and there I pitched my little tent on the tundra, not far from tree line.

My first night up there, I saw one of the most beautiful sunsets I've ever seen in my entire life, one I'll never forget, especially since a wolverine came by to see my tent, totally unafraid and more than just a little intimidating. It's said a wolverine can bring down a grown moose, so I kept my distance. It was truly a magical evening, and I felt like I lived a charmed life.

Well, that charm was about to dissipate, unbeknownst to me. I'd been up there for several days, not really doing much except enjoying the rugged beauty and making a half-hearted attempt to look for invasives, when I first heard the cries, and I'll admit, they were unsettling to the point that I immediately considered going back.

I'd been doing this job for several years, basically spending my summers out in various national parks, and I'd never heard anything like them. I wasn't sure what to think. It seemed that my idyllic life had taken a turn towards the sinister.

At first I thought they had to be some kind of distant birds calling in the night, the air currents distorting the sound, then I began to think they were wolves.

Now, my co-worker and I had been in another part of Glacier a few weeks before when we'd heard what sounded like someone hitting a tree with a baseball bat.

It was odd, and we wondered if someone was maybe lost and trying to get attention, until we heard what seemed to be a reply from some distance away, another bat hitting a tree. We decided it was hikers trying to let each other know where they were, and thought no more about it.

What gave me pause was that these cries I was now hearing seemed to be accompanied by more of this thumping sound. I found out later it's called tree knocking, but at the time, it was just plain strange—weird cries and someone whacking a tree over and over. It seemed really odd, especially out in Glacier National Park, one of the quietest and more remote areas in the country.

I'd been basing out of my tent, the tree line only fifty feet or so below me, and I liked being out in the open, as it somehow made me feel safer—you know, bears and all that.

That night, I could hear these sounds far below me, like maybe even way down on Waterton Valley Trail. Even though the cries were about as non-human sounding as could be, I decided it had to be hikers.

I had a light dinner of peanut butter and apples, then made some tea, watched the sun set over the high peaks, then went to bed, tired, thinking of when I should go back out to civilization. Since I was beginning to feel unsettled, I decided the next day would suit me just fine. I could go to Kalispell and regroup and see how my co-worker was doing.

Thinking back on it, it seems that my intuition was telling me something was afoot, even though maybe more on a subconscious level, as I wasn't really scared or anything. We would often stay out a week or more, since packing in was such a chore, and I liked getting as much done as possible while in the outback. But though I'd only been out a few days, I felt like going back, and there was nothing stopping me. I wasn't getting much done, anyway.

I was quickly asleep, tired. I woke early, just in time to watch a small herd of mountain goats make haste right by my tent in the dim light of dawn. They almost seemed as if they were running from something, as they paid me no mind. I wondered if a bear were nearby, and made sure my bear spray was handy.

I could tell from the way the clouds had moved in during the night that a storm was brewing. It made for a stunning sunrise, and I did manage to get a few photos on my little point-and-shoot camera that I used mostly for photographing plants.

Later, looking through those photos, I found I'd taken one that included the tree line, and this photo was about the only thing that made me realize I hadn't gone mad and just dreamed the whole thing.

I will add that I woke with a really uneasy feeling, then decided it was from the storm. But it was way earlier than I'm normally up, the goats waking me.

Well, since a storm was coming in, I sure didn't want to get caught up above timberline in the lightning, so I started packing up my stuff to leave. I had everything packed except my tent, which I tie onto the outside of my pack, when I heard the cries again, but this time they were much closer.

People have asked me to describe them, and it's hard, but they sounded like a mix of a wolf and a loon, yet there was something disturbingly unnatural about them, as if they were being broadcast through speakers or something, as they had a tinny sound and were really loud.

I listened, and I'll be darned if I didn't get the feeling they were triangulating my position. One would call, then another would answer, then the first, and it would have moved 30 or 40 degrees.

There were several of them, and as I stood there, mouth open, the cries sounding out sporadically, I realized the 30 and 40 degrees had become 90 and 180, and I was surrounded.

It was a creepy feeling, and I unclipped my bear spray and took off the safety, suddenly wishing I had a gun. I had no idea if these things were animal or human or large birds or something from another planet, the sounds were that unidentifiable.

Suddenly, my adrenaline kicked in, along with the famous flight or fight response. I immediately took off for the timber, angling between the sounds, leaving my somewhat expensive lightweight tent behind.

Maybe I could slip between them before they realized what was going on. It sounded like there were a couple in the trees below and maybe a couple more uphill from me in a rocky outcropping.

I hesitated for a moment, wondering if heading for the timber was the right thing to do, then I ran on, knowing it was my only hope of not being seen. I was soon in the trees, trying to be quick but quiet, making my way downhill toward the bottom of the valley where the creek was. If I could reach it, I knew I could make decent time, then get out to the Waterton Valley Trail and maybe meet up with other hikers.

I had no idea what I was running from, but my instincts said I was in danger. Keep in mind that, even though I'd left my tent behind, I was still carrying a heavy backpack, which was slowing me down, catching on the thick undergrowth and tree limbs.

I estimate I was a good half-mile from the tent when all hell broke loose. I mean, I could hear screaming and howling and carrying on like these things were right there next to me, they were so loud. And I knew they'd found my tent, intending to find me instead, and were now beyond angry. How I knew this I don't know, I just did.

I quickly took my day pack from my larger pack, put some gorp in it, along with my GPS, my maps with my research notes on them, my camera, a water bottle, some matches, and my down coat, then I ditched the big pack and started running. I've never been so terrified in my life, and it's a testament to my survival skills that I was able to think clearly enough to even grab what I did.

I could soon hear the smashing of branches and tree limbs as they came after me, and I knew there was no way I could outrun whatever it was. I still had no idea what was going on, but I felt a deep terror that drove me blindly onward.

I was following a small rivulet, which made the going somewhat easier, as it made somewhat of a path through the thick timber. I could no longer hear the sound of branches breaking, but I knew they were still coming.

As the rivulet widened, I came to a place where a small pool had formed, creating a muddy area full of some kind of tiny bird prints, maybe dippers. I don't know why, unless it was the thought that maybe these were wolves after me, but it occurred to me that I would be wise to try to mask my scent.

I knew many predators have keen senses of smell, so I stopped and began spreading mud all over myself and my pack, head to toe, as thick as possible. I then drank from my water bottle, refilled it, and quickly headed out, though first making sure I hadn't left any tracks that might identify me.

I was dripping with mud, but this was good, as it made me feel like maybe my scent wouldn't be as strong. I knew dogs rolled in carrion as a way to disguise their scent, an old remnant instinct from the days when they were wild.

Now I again heard the cries, but they sounded like they were over to my right, still in the thick timber. Had I somehow lost them? The sound was chilling, to say the least. What were they, and why were they after me?

I finally reached Valentine Creek, where I bushwhacked my way downstream until I finally reached the Waterton Valley Trail. I couldn't believe how quickly I'd come down, as it had taken me hours to get up to where I'd been camped.

I took off jogging back the way I'd come in. The Waterton Valley Trail, like its name indicated, followed along the Waterton River until it came to the ranger station and campground at Goat Haunt.

It was a long ways, and I questioned if I would ever get back, but at least now I knew I wouldn't get lost, and the odds of meeting other hikers had just increased. Safety in numbers and all that, or so I thought.

It was now early afternoon. I was exhausted, but I could think of nothing but getting back to safety. I'd left my car parked in the small town of Waterton, and once there, I could get something to eat and head back to Kalispell, or even get a motel room. But I still had miles to go, and I had no idea if these things were following me or not.

I hadn't heard any cries for some time, not since I'd gotten on the trail. I would need to get a boat at Goat Haunt, or I'd be stuck hiking back a long ways along the shore of Upper Waterton Lake. I wasn't even sure if that particular trail was accessible from Goat Haunt. Upper Waterton Lake is the largest of the three lakes and goes all the way from Glacier National Park into Canada.

I'd no more thought it than I heard a distant cry, which filled me with dread. They weren't that far behind, and they seemed to know which way I was going! I had hoped that being on a somewhat well-used trail would deter these creatures, but I was wrong.

I could no longer jog, as my sides were aching. Even at that, I'd had to stop and rest every few hundred feet, and I'd been so scared I hadn't stopped to eat or drink. I was getting fatigued beyond reason, and I knew I had to stop soon or I would collapse.

I could now see what looked like Upper Waterton Lake, but I couldn't tell what part of the long narrow lake I was seeing through the forest, whether it was near or I was seeing the far shores. For some reason, I thought that maybe when I got to Goat Haunt, I'd be safe, as there are usually a number of people camped there, plus boaters.

I heard another cry, and it was definitely closer. My heart began racing, and without even thinking it through, I diverted off the trail and scrambled down to the Waterton River. I had to stop and take a break. I was totally winded and dying of thirst.

I slid down off the riverbank to the edge of the shallow water. That late in the season, I could easily wade across the river if need be.

The mud I'd plastered all over myself was dried and caking off, and I needed a fresh supply to cloak my scent, but I needed food and water and rest even more. But I knew that hiding my scent was of paramount importance, so I quickly again rubbed mud all over myself from head to toe.

Another cry, and now much closer! It sounded so full of hatred, or was I just imagining it? Had I somehow intruded on their territory? Why were they after me?

Now walking along the bank, I spotted a large tree whose roots had been exposed where the bank was eroding away, creating a small hole. I quickly made my way to it, hoping it might provide a place to hide.

It was tight, but I managed to cram myself back into the hole, basically up behind the mass of roots. I felt I was well-hidden, yet I could still see out somewhat. It was dank and claustrophobic feeling, but maybe I could rest here, drink some water and eat some of the gorp in my small pack, then again head back down the trail.

I dearly wanted to get to Goat Haunt before dark, especially since I'd forgotten my headlamp. The idea of spending the night out in the cold and uncertainty wasn't a pleasant one, I can tell you that.

I pulled my down coat from my pack, glad I'd had the presence of mind to stuff it in there. Putting it on, I knew it would help keep me warm if I did have to spend the night, plus its dark green color was good for helping me blend into the riverbank. The only bad thing was that it wasn't covered with mud, and I worried that it carried my scent. I grabbed a handful of dirt and rubbed it on the coat.

I then ate several handfuls of trail mix, emptied my water bottle, and basically passed out from exhaustion. When I woke it was dusk, and I panicked, but then settled down, realizing I was in a good place and would be better off sleeping through the night and starting out when I was rested and it was daylight. Plus, these things would hopefully be long gone by then. They obviously hadn't found me, and it had been a few hours, so maybe they'd gone on back.

I couldn't see them wanting to go near human habitation, where they were likely to get shot. And as I dozed back off, I again wished I had a gun, my bear spray handy.

I awoke in the night, chilly but somewhat rested. I was feeling better, but was getting thirsty again and my water bottle was empty. The river was nearby, but I was too afraid to leave my hiding place so stayed put, and it wasn't long until the gurgling of the water lulled me back to sleep.

I suddenly awoke, terrified, for something with sharp claws was grabbing at my pant leg. I was afraid to move, but in the dim light of dawn I could see a small pair of beady eyes looking up at me.

It was a pine marten! I'd seen these small animals many times in Glacier. They seemed very intelligent and fed on fish, insects, and vegetation. It seemed totally unafraid of me, and sat there as if waiting for something. Maybe I'd invaded its nest, I thought, and it was waiting for me to leave.

It was then that I heard something nearby, something that was making no effort at all to be stealthy and quiet. The marten now crawled up behind me into the hood of my coat, and I knew it was hiding. Whatever was out there, it was more frightened of it than it was of me.

I know bears will eat pine martins when they can catch them, though it was rare, so I suspected it was a bear foraging about. But suddenly a strong smell drifted in, and I knew it wasn't a bear. Bears can smell pretty gnarly, but this thing smelled more like a pit toilet. It was all I could do to not gag, and I slowly put my hands over my nose, trying to break the smell's potency.

I couldn't see much through the tangle of roots, but I definitely smelled something, and my senses were totally overwhelmed to the point that I wanted nothing more than to flee. I began quietly taking deep breaths, trying to still my fears. The little pine marten hidden down in my hood made no movement at all.

It seems like I sat there stiff and cold for an eternity, but I must've gone back to sleep. When I woke, I could see the light glow on the river from the dawn. I could barely move, but I reached up and felt the hood of my coat. The pine marten was gone. This was a good sign.

I listened for the longest time, afraid that whatever had been there was still waiting. Finally, when the sun began to break through the trees and the birds started chirping, I realized that there was probably nothing out there.

It was all I could do to pull myself from behind the root ball, I was so stiff and sore, but I was soon down by the river, filling my water bottle and drinking. At that point, it was a choice between getting giardia and dying of dehydration. I drank several bottles, downed the rest of my gorp, then pulled myself up the bank and back onto the trail.

People asked me later if I found any tracks, which would have helped me identify what was out there, but in all honesty, I was too tired to even think to look. All I cared about was getting to Goat Haunt, and I was so sore from spending the night basically half-standing that it seemed like an iffy proposition to do even that.

But as I stumbled down the trail, I began to loosen up and was soon making pretty good time. The little bit of sunlight that had lit up the river was now just a memory, as the sun was now hidden behind dark and menacing-looking clouds.

I was still wearing my down coat, and I knew the coat would be useless if it got wet, as it wasn't waterproof. My waterproof shell was back in my pack, somewhere above Valentine Creek. I knew I needed to hurry.

It seemed like it took forever, but I finally reached Goat Haunt, to my relief. The campground was empty except for one youngish looking backpacker ready to head up the trail, a single fellow with a pack so big it towered over his head. Keep in mind that it was September, which is nearly winter in the Canadian Rockies. You'll meet day hikers, but rarely do backpackers go out then, as the weather's too iffy, with deep snows not unusual.

When he saw me, he came over to talk, giving me the strangest look and asking if I was OK.

I'd forgotten I was caked in mud and dirt. I wasn't sure what to say

—I mean, I could lie and said I'd fallen or something, but could I live with myself if I didn't tell this young guy what had happened? He was alone, and therefore more vulnerable. The park rangers in both Waterton and Glacier always discourage people from going out alone, especially backpacking.

I decided to level with him. I told him why I was caked in mud, where I'd spent the night, and all about the cries and smells and the feeling that I was being hunted.

By the time I'd finished, he'd taken his pack off and leaned it against a tree, looking concerned. When I told him I was a park botanist, that seemed to add the credibility my story needed, and as he hoisted his pack back on, he said he was going out with me.

His name was John, and we got to be friends. He later told me he'd been feeling uncertain about his hike ever since the previous night, as if intuition was telling him not to go, plus the weather looked sketchy. The ranger at the station there had also tried to discourage him.

I can't tell you how happy I was to have someone with me, but the clincher was that even though we wanted to get to Waterton, there was no way to get there. The ranger station was closed, and there was no one else around. We sat there at a picnic table for some time, listening for the sound of a boat motor, but no one came.

After we'd sat there for some time, John grabbed me by the arm. He motioned for me to listen, and there, in the distance, were the cries again. He looked white as a sheet.

I panicked. Where could we go? These creatures seemed to have figured out where I'd gone, for the sounds weren't all that far away.

To our relief, it was then that a park boat came along, a ranger coming out to check on things. He docked the boat and had soon opened the ranger station, where we went inside.

I really don't recall much of what was said, as I was so fatigued and disoriented from a lack of sleep, but I do recall John and I taking the ranger back outside, where we sat for awhile, listening, the ranger looking skeptical.

Sure enough, more cries, and they were even closer, and now the ranger looked worried. He decided it would be prudent for us all to get back to Waterton, especially given the incoming weather. We boarded the boat, and I'll never forget reaching the end of the lower lake, the distant sight of the Prince of Wales Hotel up on the hill above town welcoming us back to civilization.

Once back in Waterton, I got a room and cleaned up as best as I could, trying to rub off all the mud. And even though the ranger we'd met knew my story, I decided to go to the Waterton Lakes National Park offices there and meet with the ranger on duty.

I wanted them to know what had happened for several reasons, but primarily so they would be aware that the pack and tent were mine, in case someone reported a missing person. I didn't have much hope of ever getting them back, for even if no one bothered them, being out all winter would pretty much cause them to deteriorate.

The ranger knew me from my job, so he wasn't as skeptical as I had anticipated. He simply said he'd had other reports from up there, but no one had actually been threatened like I had. He told me he hadn't believed the reports until then, and now he was starting to wonder, but wasn't sure what to do.

I called my supervisor, telling her I was out and that I'd be back at Glacier headquarters the next day and would meet with her. Once there, I told her the exact same story. Like the Waterton ranger, she was skeptical, yet listened. And since it was so close to the end of the season, she said I could finish my plant maps and report and call it a year, which I did.

I spent a few days in Kalispell visiting my co-worker, who was doing well, telling him the story, and I know it scared him to death. Neither of us ever went back to Glacier, instead working the next season down in Texas in Big Bend National Park, then at various other places.

The guy I met at the campground and I stay in touch, and he's told me more than once that I saved his life, though neither of us know what would've actually happened had he gone on. He may have been fine, or maybe the weather would've turned him around before anything happened, as it snowed two feet in Waterton that night. But those cries we heard indicate otherwise.

Strangely enough, someone did find my pack the next spring, and it was pretty much intact. I asked the park service to keep it, for I'd replaced everything in it by then, except for a small hand-held digital recorder that I sometimes used to take notes while in the field. I asked them to send that to me, though I was doubtful it would still work after being out all winter, though it was secure in a waterproof case inside the pack.

When I got it back, I replaced the batteries, and sure enough, it still worked. I listened to my ramblings for awhile, notes to myself about plants and what I was seeing, then it simply went quiet. It was as if the recorder had been on but no one was saying anything. I found that odd, but not really indicative of anything.

But when I was going through my photos later, I found those I'd taken just before abandoning my tent and running away. Most weren't worth keeping, but there was one of the edge of the forest with something that looked odd. I zoomed in and studied it for awhile. What I saw gave me the chills, even though it was indistinct and hard to make out.

There, right along the tree line, looking out at me, was a huge blob-like thing, something very large and very black, and the camera had picked up a glare that looked like it had red eyeshine. There was no way it was a bear, for it had large and very long arms and shoulders that made it look like it could pick up a Volkswagen.

Not long after that, I got a call from the same park ranger at Waterton who'd taken us out by boat. He told me they'd found my tent, and it was ripped to shreds.

I wasn't surprised by this, though it did make the hair on my neck stand up. But when he told me three other hikers had seen several what he called Sasquatch up under Porcupine Ridge on the Boulder Pass Trail, which is near where I'd been camped, I knew I hadn't gone crazy, even though I'd wondered about my sanity since then. They hadn't been approached by the creatures and had immediately left the park.

Would I tell people to *not* backpack in Glacier? No, it's just too beautiful to not see, at least once in one's lifetime, but I would definitely never go alone. But if you do, don't forget my mudpack trick, for I really do think it's what saved my life, as I know it made it harder for them to track me.

But basically, just take my advice and don't go alone.

12

THE FIDDLER ON THE DECK

[Like the previous account, this story is also from my "Montana Bigfoot Campfire Stories." Once again, I'm including it here in case you haven't read it, as it took place near Glacier.]

I met Orin when guiding a fishing trip in my home state of Colorado. He'd been given the trip for his 50th birthday as a gift from his wife and kids, and he sure seemed to be enjoying himself. He and his wife owned a small ranch not too far away, where they raised alpacas in the shadow of magnificent Mt. Sopris, selling the wool to weavers.

We were fishing the Frying Pan River, one of the state's premier trout fisheries, when we heard a noise in the thick brush along the creek. I laughed when Orin said it was maybe a Bigfoot.

It turned out to be a deer, but I later asked him if he believed in Bigfoot. He said he did and later told the following story over one of my traditional Dutch-oven dinners, a story that I found to be both moving and poignant. It gave me real insight into the kind of guy he was, and he's someone I now value as a friend. —Rusty

. . .

R usty, my name's Orin and I come from a long line of musicians. My grandfather played cello with the Boston Philharmonic, and my grandmother played harp for private events, you know, like weddings and such, all in Boston. Their daughter, my mom, played piano and later harp, then moved to Montana for college, of all places, where she met my dad.

My dad's side was also musical, but they came from the Missouri Ozarks and had their own ideas about the subject. My dad played dobro and guitar. I'm always amazed when I think of how different my mom and dad were, but they say opposites attract.

In any case, I grew up in the middle of all this, in rural Montana, listening to my mom play classical piano and harp and my dad play bluegrass dobro and country guitar—oh, and he also played a mean harmonica.

My older sister took lessons from my mom and became a pretty good pianist herself, sometimes playing for school events, church, that kind of thing, but never professionally. I grew up refusing to play anything, always the rebel, though I did once threaten to take up bagpipes when my mom wouldn't leave me alone about taking lessons.

But I always liked music, as long as it wasn't classical or bluegrass —or folk, I hated folk. So what did that leave? Rock and roll, baby. But the closest I ever got to playing rock and roll was on my stereo.

If they had an award for disappointing your parents, I'd be first in line. I not only refused to play an instrument, I also refused to go to college. My dad didn't really care, as he'd dropped out of college and was a lineman, but it basically killed my mom, for she had a university education, as did her entire family. Like I said, how those two ever got together is a mystery.

Instead of being a doctor or such like my mom wanted, I became a finish carpenter. I love working with wood, and there are lots of nice houses near Kalispell with beautiful custom cabinets and such that have my signature on them—well, not literally, but my work really stands out. I hope I don't sound like a braggart, but I guess I still feel a little insecure about not being a professional with a college degree—thanks to my mom, though I love her dearly. Oh, and my sis became a dentist, so I should thank her, too, I guess.

But I was the one who got to live on the edge of some of the most beautiful wild country in the United States, maybe all of North America, because I built my own house on 80 acres I'd bought back before things got so expensive.

Where was it? Right on the boundary of Glacier National Park near West Glacier, Montana. I got to live in a landscape that a lot of people only dream of. My wife and I had a house that wasn't just beautiful inside, but beautiful in every direction you looked. It was like living in a landscape painting. My sis lives in a fancy subdivision in Denver, with her neighbor's fence for a view.

Living close to nature is good for you. When I die, I want my obit to read something like, "He always lived in the most beautiful places," just like the one for the famous artist Russell Chatham read. Chatham also lived in Montana.

Well, they say you always eventually go home, and when you get older, I think it's true, you go back to what you grew up with. And for me, that was music.

I was in my early 40s, and I'd finally got to the place where I could afford to take some time off now and then. My wife, Becky, worked in the billing office of a medical clinic, and her income gave us some stability, so I didn't worry when I was between jobs.

Actually, my work was more and more in demand as wealthy people discovered the area, and I was keeping really busy. I'd just finished a big job, an expensive house owned by a celebrity singer down in Lakeside, and I needed a break.

So, I took a month off and just kicked back, taking it easy, working on some projects around the house, cooking a lot—I love to cook—cleaning and doing the laundry, and taking care of our two kids, though being in high school, neither required much care. Becky got to where she hoped I wouldn't go back to work, as she now had a house-husband, but after a week I started getting bored.

One day I'd gone to downtown Kalispell for something or other, and I happened to notice a pawn shop. I'm all for a bargain, so I went inside, and there, lo and behold, was a violin!

I stood there, dumbfounded, as a whole host of feelings came from nowhere, feelings of nostalgia and of visiting my grandparents in their big old Boston house when I was a kid, them serenading us on the cello and harp.

I didn't even think about it, I just bought the darn thing and walked out the door, no idea what I was going to do with it.

Well, what I did with it was become obsessed. I guess all those musical genes raised their ugly heads, because all I wanted to do was learn to play that darn violin. I couldn't read a lick of music, so I took it up by ear, and I will say I seemed to have a bit of talent for it, as it came pretty easily, and I knew violin wasn't an easy instrument to learn.

But I didn't want to learn to play violin, I wanted to learn to play the fiddle. For all practical purposes, they're the same instrument, the terms just referring to how you play it—violin is classical, while fiddle is bluegrass.

Growing up in rural Montana, you don't hear much classical music, and there can be a bit of a highbrow association with it. And even though I seemed to be going back to my musical roots, I had no intention of playing classical, as I hadn't lost my mind, not yet, anyway. It was too hard and too stuffy and formal for my tastes.

I just wanted to play fiddle. I'd apparently lost my dislike of blue-grass. I bought a couple of books, but I don't remember even reading them, I just practiced and practiced.

Well, as far as Becky was concerned, I might've just started drink-ing, though fiddle playing was a lot more intrusive. I'm not saying she wasn't supportive, as she was, but she was much more supportive when I didn't practice where she could hear me. So, I played in the basement, spending every spare minute practicing. Maybe I would've been better off drinking—it's not as noisy.

Well, my wife was probably wondering what next, but she had no idea. I started getting interested in venues where people played fiddle. I say venues, but I didn't care whether it was something like the Red Ants Pants Music Festival over by White Sulphur Springs or an open mic at the local bar. I just wanted to hear other people play the fiddle and see how they did it. It was like learning a foreign language—full immersion is the best.

I started going out a lot. I think Becky at first thought I was having a mid-life crises, and maybe I was, but it wasn't your usual kind. I'd sometimes take the kids with me, or sometimes Becky would go, or I'd go alone, I didn't care.

I'd talk to the musicians and see how they did things. Becky said I should get a job covering the music beat for the paper, and I was so nuts I actually considered it for a minute, even though I'm not much of a writer.

I finally got a job doing cabinets in a new house over in Columbia Falls, but even on my breaks I'd play that darn fiddle. I was actually getting to where I could play some tunes pretty good, or at least that's what my daughter Kim told me.

Well, one evening after work I got tired of the basement and took my fiddle out onto the back deck. Like I said, we had 80 acres, and it was mostly thick timber, but you could see the tall mountains of Glacier in the distance.

While out there playing, I felt different. I realized I felt free and unfettered, and after that, I'd play out on the deck as long as the weather allowed, even at night.

You can probably see where this is going. Playing out in nature, I was sure to become a curiosity for whatever was around, and that's exactly what happened. Animals are smart, and it behooves them to know what's in their environment. They're naturally curious.

I found that, if I played during the day, the squirrels and birds would come around as if to listen. In the evening, it would be the deer and an occasional fox or coyote. But I wasn't really prepared for what eventually came around.

I like Irish music, and I was getting to where I could play some jigs and reels and that kind of thing. Irish music is hard to play, so I must have been getting better. A lot of bluegrass has its origins in Irish and Scottish music.

Part of what I liked about it was that it was so lively and fun. So, I'd be out there on our back deck stomping around and playing some enthusiastic bluegrass, all caught up in it, and then look up to see I had an audience—a couple of deer, maybe a few bluejays, a rabbit, that kind of thing, though usually not at the same time.

If the weather was nice, I'd sometimes do a barbecue for dinner and Becky and the kids would come out and listen to me play while eating. I would play quieter music then so as to not run them off, stuff like ballads, that same folk music I'd always hated.

By then, Becky was starting to appreciate my efforts more, and she'd sit and listen, saying it was all so lovely, music out in the woods. This made me feel really good, and I started to get an inkling of why my mom's family had loved music so much.

Well, barbecue and bluegrass, what could go better together? Apparently, we weren't the only ones who liked that combination. I think it was the smell of the barbecue that first brought my new audience to me, but I do think the music helped keep them around.

But I'm getting ahead of myself.

One evening, I'd pretty much played myself out, and it was getting late. I was sitting in one of the deck chairs, and my daughter Kim came out and joined me. We talked about school and her future plans and life in general, and she finally told me, "Dad, you're getting pretty good on that thing. I really admire your ability to focus and stick with something so hard."

I was pleased to hear it, telling her that maybe someday I'd be good enough to play in front of a real audience, like at the Red Ants Pants. She'd gone with me not long before, and we'd both really enjoyed it.

I was surprised by her reply.

"Don't do it, Dad. The pressure just ruins it. That's why I quit drama. I love acting, but having an audience changes everything. It's no longer fun."

I knew she'd quit her high-school drama class, but I hadn't known why until then.

"Some people love an audience," I replied. "It motivates them to do even better, and creates a kind of synergy."

"I know," she replied. "But Dad, I know you too well. You're not going to like it. Like you always tell us, know thyself."

Ah, the wisdom of children. I wish I'd listened, but instead, a seed had been planted. I wanted to join a group. Maybe I actually was reliving my younger days, or at least I knew Becky thought so.

Before I knew it, I'd managed to hook up with several other guys who had the same idea. We said our main goal was to have fun, but I knew that in the back of all of our minds we wanted to play semi-professionally, or at least in front of a real audience. And, of course, since I lived out in the woods, it made sense for us to practice on our back deck.

And man, did we have fun. We had one guy on the guitar, one on harmonica, one on steel guitar, and me on fiddle. Our guitar player also sang, and I did backup vocals, discovering that I had a pretty nice tenor voice, or at least that's what the guys told me. We'd do a potluck barbecue on Friday evenings after work, then play until we could play no more. It got to where their spouses, friends, kids, you name it would come along, and it eventually turned into one big party, every Friday night.

Well, one summer night, everyone had gone home except Wes, my buddy who played guitar, and we were sitting around in the dark, winding down and talking.

Wes was feeling like we'd reached a dead end with the band, and he wanted to branch out. I was surprised, thinking we were just getting going good, but he wanted to start playing more Western tunes. He wanted me to sing more lead, as he felt I had a good voice and it would add variety. He said I should learn to yodel.

I got a good laugh from this, I can tell you, and as we sat there talking, I felt a sense of nostalgia come over me, a farawayness, like I was suddenly a part of something bigger than me.

I looked out at the dark forest all around us, only half listening to Wes talk about some guy he'd met called Wiley who had a band called Wiley and the Wild West. They sang authentic old tunes like *Cattle Call* and *Red River Valley*. Wiley was apparently a rancher out by the Highline in the central part of the state, called that because it was the northern route of the Burlington Northern Railroad.

The more Wes talked, the more I felt like I was being transported into a different life and time, and I could now picture myself walking with a band of people, long ago, like some tribe, and these were my own relatives, my own kind, and we lived right here in the high mountains of Glacier and had for many millennia. It was almost like a vision.

Wes was now going on and on about how we could do Wiley and the Wild West kind of stuff, but I really needed to learn how to yodel, as that was part of the old Western style of singing, and I definitely had the voice for it, having a high range and all. He knew he could get us gigs, maybe even some festivals.

But I wasn't listening, for I could now see some of my people standing at the forest's edge in the darkness, not far away at all, and they were somehow beckoning me to join them, saying I didn't belong where I was and would be much happier with them, living as I was meant to live as my kind had for thousands, maybe millions of years.

Wes was now irritated, and his sharp voice brought me back to reality. I assured him I'd been listening and would consider it all, and I thought changing from bluegrass to authentic Western would be a great thing, even though I barely knew what I was saying.

Wes had to go home, but I suddenly wanted him to stay. I felt like I was losing my sense of boundaries, who I was, and there was something out there I didn't understand.

I, of course, didn't say anything about all this to him, I just tried to get him to talk more about yodeling. But he stood to go, saying his wife would be worrying about him if he was very late, and besides, for some reason, he felt uncomfortable out here in the dark, like maybe there was a bear out there or something.

I followed him inside, locking the door, then turning on the deck lights. Becky was watching some TV show and the kids were upstairs, and I wanted desperately to get everyone together, as if there was some natural disaster about to happen. I almost felt panicked.

I figured it was something mental going on, maybe discomfort from Wes talking about playing in big venues and all, so I went back into the kitchen and got a beer, thinking it would settle my nerves.

As I stood there, I looked out the window at the edge of the forest, and I swear I could see eyes shining in the dark. I sometimes would see eyeshine from deer and elk and other animals if they passed through the outside lights, but this was different because it was a good six feet or more off the ground and nowhere near the lights— and the eyes were red as blood.

I was stunned and went back into the living room. I never drink late at night like that, and Becky noticed, asking if I was OK. I told her I felt weird and had just seen strange eyes looking at the house from the forest. She laughed, went into the kitchen to look, then came back to her TV show, saying it had to be my imagination and maybe I shouldn't be drinking beer.

I went upstairs and looked out from our bedroom window, but saw nothing. We have a nice recliner there for reading, and I crawled onto that, pulled a blanket up over my face, and promptly went to sleep.

I dreamed—or was it a dream?—that I was again with my people, and we were traversing a large glacier, careful to not fall into a crevasse, and it was all very tense. We were fleeing from something, and my mother held my hand tightly, telling me not to look back. My father was ahead of us, and he carried a spear and was dressed in a huge black robe, and it was then I looked back. In the distance was a creature with a coat just like the robe, and I knew my father had killed one and made a coat from it.

I woke, half sick, and it took me forever to realize where I was. Becky was in bed sleeping and had left the night light on.

I got up and quietly walked to the bedroom window, looking out again at the forest, but saw nothing. It was four a.m., and there was no way I was going to be able to sleep, so I went downstairs and made a pot of coffee and started a batch of cinnamon rolls. Like I said, I liked to cook—it relaxed me, and boy, did I ever need relaxing after that dream.

I wanted to go drink my coffee on the deck and watch the stars, which I often did when getting up early, though my normal time was around six, nor four. But I was afraid, so I went back to the living room.

I sat there sipping my hot coffee, thinking. What was going on? It was then that I remembered the DNA test Becky had wanted me to take, thinking it would be fun for the kids to know more about their genetics. I'd laughed it off, knowing there's a lot of controversy about the accuracy of such things. Becky had found it funny when mine had come back with the results saying I was four percent Neanderthal.

Kim had later done some research, telling me that being Neanderthal wasn't at all what I'd thought and that a lot of people had Neanderthal genes. Archeologists were now finding evidence that the Neanderthal had been artistic and musical, and they believed that they had blue eyes and red hair. Kim said that maybe I should be proud of my Neanderthal blood, as it maybe helped make me a better musician. I liked her theory and found it somewhat comforting.

But archaeologists also believe that the Neanderthal were killed off by Homo sapiens, even though there had been some interbreeding. Was this the source of the dreams? Were we fleeing from a Neanderthal?

It didn't seem right, and what about the red eyeshine I'd seen? Did it have anything to do with the dream?

The cinnamon rolls were done and the sun was rising, so I took a roll and another cup of coffee out to the back deck. I was feeling much better, now fully awake, one good cup of coffee already in me and a hot cinnamon roll wafting its yummy smell, and for no reason at all, I remembered what Wes had said the night before.

I started yodeling—well, my idea of yodeling, I should say. What I lacked in technique I made up for in volume, the sound reverberating off the nearby hills. I was impressed at how loud it sounded, but then again, I'd never tried yodeling off the deck before. I hoped I hadn't wakened Becky and the kids. For some reason, maybe in contrast to the dream, it felt like a new start, a new day, and I felt optimism and even joy.

I was happy to not be that kid hurrying across the glacier, being chased by something ominous, but instead here in beautiful Montana with a beautiful family and nice house and stunning landscape to look at whenever I wanted, and heck, I even liked my job. Life couldn't get any better.

Well, that's when the yodel came back to me, and no, it wasn't an echo. But it didn't sound human, nor was it really a yodel, but more of a strange yell coming from up the mountainside.

I quickly went back inside, shocked. In all the years we'd lived there, I'd never heard anything like that. And no, it wasn't a mountain lion, I'd heard plenty of those, as well as bobcat screams and even bears and coyotes making strange noises, as well as odd-sounding birds.

I again thought of the dream, and I somehow wondered if it was related. I again had the urge to gather my family and our two cats and flee, but now it was broad daylight, so it had nothing to do with strange night fears.

Becky was now up, having coffee and a roll, and I asked her if she'd heard anything. She hadn't, but wanted to go out on the deck and listen, intrigued by my description.

And of course we heard nothing out there at all. But we did have a nice discussion about moving into town, one instigated by me. Becky said I needed to get out of the house, and since it was Saturday, once the kids were up, we all went into Kalispell, where we had lunch and did a little shopping out at the mall north of town. I wanted to drive around a few neighborhoods, which made Becky realize that I was somewhat serious about moving.

I found several places I liked, but none had the views and privacy our place had. But now Becky started getting into the idea, as it would make work much closer for her, as she worked there in town. The kids were more hesitant, as it would mean changing schools, though neither had long until they were in college, and Kalispell has a community college they could both attend for their first two years, saving a bundle on tuition and other costs.

The idea was beginning to jell, and all because of red eyeshine, a dream, and an odd yell, none of which had been more than 24 hours earlier. I thought of all the work I'd put into our place, all the custom this and that, and I started feeling a sense of regret for having said anything. But we'd lived in the same place since before the kids were born, and we could get a fortune for it, especially with all that land, so maybe it wasn't such a bad idea.

But now Becky was saying something about how maybe we should leave Montana and try someplace new where we could buy a ranch for what our place was worth, like Wyoming or Nebraska. I knew she was thinking of her lifelong dream to live on a ranch like the one she'd grown up on instead of dealing with Medicare and Medicaid billing and non-paying patients all day long.

I couldn't believe where a weird dream and some strangeness was now heading. I loved Montana and never wanted to leave, it was where I'd been born and raised, and I was seriously regretting having said anything. Moving to a different property was one thing, but leaving Montana?

That evening, back on the deck, I was looking at things with new eyes, as if I'd just moved there, seeing it for what it was. They say you don't appreciate what you have until it's gone, and I didn't want that to happen. I wanted to look at what we had through unbiased eyes before we made any decisions. Sure, it had been my idea, but I now felt I'd been operating from a position of irrational fear.

I surveyed the scene—a beautiful pristine forest with wildlife galore, many who came to visit in the evening hours, unafraid. There were a number of animal trails we could walk in total peace and privacy, though we didn't go out there as much as we'd done when the kids were little, exploring and enjoying nature. And we even had our own small stream that coursed down through the forest from the big hills above us.

If I stood up or looked out from the upstairs windows, I could even see some of the high peaks in Glacier National Park towering high above with their snowcapped tops, a sight many would pay a fortune to have. And it was all so peaceful.

And what about the house? I'd built it with my own two hands while Becky and I lived in a small trailer. The cabinets were custom birch, and the ceilings were custom woods from a reclaimed flour mill over on the plains. Everything was handmade, and based on the praise I'd received over the years, well done. How could we ever sell it?

I felt a poignancy, a feeling that something important was about to be lost, and I went back inside. I needed to talk to Becky.

But when I saw her on her computer looking at some land agency's listings, I felt selfish and defeated. Maybe we should move for her sake. Sure, I'd built up a reputation as a finish carpenter, but I could rebuild that, even if we weren't in a well-heeled place. Becky had always been there for me, working hard at a job she really didn't like, and maybe it was time to give her a break. I just couldn't believe how fast things were moving.

That night, I had another dream. I was no longer a child, but I was still with my people, and now I was the one wearing the dark skin. I didn't really want to wear it, but my father was dead, killed by one of the black creatures. I now had to follow tradition and wear the robe.

And now, that creature's kin wanted to kill me. I could hear them in the nearby forest, talking in their strange language, and I knew they were coming for me.

All I wanted was to stop this killing and retribution. Why couldn't we live in peace? We were different, yet we had many similarities—we had language, loved our families, and ate the same plants and fish and small animals. It seemed we had much in common, so why fight? And I somehow knew my species would win in the end, decimating theirs, and this made me sad,

even though they'd killed my father. I knew they were no Neanderthal.

Then, still dreaming, I wondered, did they have music? Did their
brains process sound the same way ours did? Could their ears hear
the many changes in pitch ours did? I'd read that humans can easily
detect frequencies as fine as one twelfth of an octave—a half step in
musical terminology—but predatory species such as dogs can only
discriminate one third of an octave, and even our primate relatives
could only hear changes of half an octave.

Were these black creatures primates like us? They had to be.
Maybe music could be our common language, a way to communi-
cate our fears and dreams to each other, and then we'd stop
fighting.

I now dreamed that I took out a simple flute I'd carved and
started playing. But they were still stalking me, and I stopped playing,
getting my spear ready.

I woke, immediately knowing I'd been dreaming and yet afraid
anyway. It all seemed too real, but Becky was beside me, sound
asleep. It was four a.m., just like before.

I quietly got up and slipped on my clothes, then went downstairs
to the kitchen, again making coffee. We still had some scones from
the bakery in Kalispell the day before, so I grabbed one and went
back on the deck, even though it was still pitch dark. I knew I had to
confront my fears.

And there, again, like before, was something standing at the edge
of the trees, something with glowing red eyes. I was scared to death
and went back inside, but then I decided to get my fiddle. The dream
had planted a thought—could music be a bridge between different
species? I didn't even know what species I was looking at, but it was
worth a try. Instead of running like a scared rabbit, I would give it a
shot.

I began playing quietly, so as not to wake Becky and the kids, but
hopefully loud enough that whatever was out there would hear me. I
started out with an old Scottish song about the heather in the high-
lands and pining for a lost love, then segued into a beautiful Robert

Burns song with Gaelic lyrics I didn't understand, something about calling the sheep.

I next thought of Wes and his desire to play old cowboy songs, so I played a song called *Twilight on the Trail*, then went into an old tune called the *Rose Blossom Special*. I must say I surprised myself at how many songs I actually knew.

And as I played, I wondered if whatever was out there would hear things the same way I did. Maybe they hated music and would run away.

When I finally looked up, the eyeshine was gone, but in its place were three shadows, and I thought at first they were bears, but soon realized I was looking at the same type of creatures I'd seen in my dreams. They were much closer, seemingly entranced by my playing.

It was almost dawn, just light enough to see them, and even though I knew I should be afraid, I wasn't, for I knew they wouldn't harm me. They nodded their heads as if asking for more, so I stood and played my heart out, every song I knew, from Marty Robbins to Blue Rodeo to Driftwood Holly and songs I've now long forgotten.

As the sun rose, they faded back into the trees, gone like a dream. And later that night, once it was again dark, I went back out onto the deck to find a beautiful bunch of colorful river stones on the steps, and I somehow knew they'd left them.

That same day, I called a land conservation agency and asked about putting most of our land into a perpetual conservancy, leaving only a couple of acres out for the house. I was worried that it would greatly decrease the amount we'd get from the property, but the guy there said it usually had the opposite effect, that it made it more desirable because the taxes were much lower and people liked knowing it would never be developed.

I talked to Becky and she was all for it, so we proceeded. After that was put into place, our next step was to call a real-estate agent and list the property. We were both astounded by what they suggested we list it for. Because it backed to Glacier National Park, it was worth a fortune, and we had several offers the week it was listed.

After we sold it, I was sitting on the back deck one last time, as we would leave the next morning, most of our stuff already moved to the place we'd rented in Kalispell until we could decide where to go next.

I'd left the band, no longer having any desire to play for an audience, for who could ever best the one I'd just played for?

There on the deck, I took out my fiddle and played an old Bob Marley tune, singing quietly, "Every little thing's gonna be alright."

I sat for awhile, enjoying the quiet, then went inside, turning off the deck lights for the last time.

ABOUT THE AUTHOR

Rusty Wilson is a fly-fishing guide based in Colorado and Montana. He's well-known for his Dutch-oven cookouts and campfires, where he's heard some pretty wild stories about the creatures in the woods, especially Bigfoot.

Whether you're a Bigfoot believer or not, we hope you enjoyed this book, and we know you'll enjoy Rusty's many others, the first of which is *Rusty Wilson's Bigfoot Campfire Stories.* Also check out Rusty's bestselling *Yellowstone Bigfoot Campfire Stories,* as well as *Bigfoot: The Dark Side, The Creature of Lituya Bay,* and *Chasing After Bigfoot: My Search for North America's Most Elusive Creature.*

Rusty's books come in ebook format, as well as in print and audio.

You'll also enjoy the first book in the Bud Shumway mystery series, a Bigfoot mystery, *The Ghost Rock Cafe.*

Other offerings from Yellow Cat Publishing include an RV series by RV expert Sunny Skye, which includes *Living the Simple RV Life.* And don't forget to check out the books by Sunny's friend, Bob Davidson: *On the Road with Joe,* and *Any Road, USA.* And finally, you'll love Roger Dean Miller's comedy thriller, *Bombing Hoffman.*

Made in the USA
Las Vegas, NV
23 June 2021